Different Days

Different Days

Vicki Berger Erwin

Sky Pony Press
New York

First Edition

This is a work of fiction. Names, characters, places, and incidents are from the author's imagination and used fictitiously.

Sky Pony Press books may be purchased in bulk at special discounts for sales promotion, corporate gifts, fund-raising, or educational purposes. Special editions can also be created to specifications. For details, contact the Special Sales Department, Sky Pony Press, 307 West 36th Street, 11th Floor, New York, NY 10018 or info@skyhorsepublishing.com.

Sky Pony® is a registered trademark of Skyhorse Publishing, Inc.®, a Delaware corporation.

www.skyponypress.com
www.vickibergererwin.com

10 9 8 7 6 5 4 3 2 1

Library of Congress Cataloging-in-Publication Data is available on file.

Cover design by Sammy Yuen
Cover illustration copyright © 2017 by Scott Altmann

Print ISBN: 978-1-5107-2458-7
Ebook ISBN: 978-1-5107-2463-1

Printed in the United States of America

For Doris Berg Nye and her family,
whose brave lives and actions inspired Rosie's story

No free man shall be seized, or imprisoned, or disseized of land,
Or outlawed, or in any way destroyed;
Nor will we condemn him, nor will we commit him to prison,
Excepting by the legal judgment of his peers, or by the laws of the land.
— Magna Carta, Article 39, the basis of
the United States Constitution

Chapter 1

Oahu, Territory of Hawaii, December 7, 1941

Rosie could read the funnies for herself and had been able to since she was four. But sitting on the arm of Papa's easy chair, leaning into him, and laughing together at Nancy and Sluggo or L'il Abner on Sunday morning was one of her favorite parts of the week.

The sweet smell of baking muffins drifting from the kitchen made her stomach growl and her mouth water as she listened with one ear for Mama to call them to breakfast.

Rosie felt the *BOOM!* of an explosion almost before she heard it. She had to wrap her arm around Papa's neck to keep from tumbling off the arm of the chair.

Papa dropped the newspaper and the two of them sat, frozen, as more explosions rocked the house. Rosie covered her ears against the noise.

"What was that?" her little brother Freddie yelled from his room across the hall.

Rosie and Papa exchanged glances as Rosie jumped up and crossed to the window in two leaps, her father right behind her. Huge columns of black smoke boiled over the island between their home and Pearl Harbor. More explosions shook the house and rattled the windows.

"A fuel tank exploding, perhaps?" Papa murmured, almost to himself.

Rosie nodded. *Yes*, she thought, *a fuel tank*. There had been explosions before, but this one felt different—bigger, for sure. And the blasts didn't stop. Rosie flinched as still another *BOOM!* rocked the house.

Leaving Papa at the window, Rosie ran down the stairs and out into the yard. The clouds of thick, black mushrooming smoke grew and crept slowly away from the harbor as Rosie continued to feel and hear one blast after another until they seemed to run together. The smell was faint, but ugly. She wrinkled her nose. Feeling a tug on her arm, Rosie looked down. Freddie pointed overhead.

Rosie followed the direction of his finger and stared, not exactly sure what she was seeing. A plane flew low against the blue sky dimmed by smoke, so low she could see into the cockpit—the pilot's face half covered with goggles and the scarf tied around his neck. The plane was not like any she had seen on maneuvers from the nearby air bases. This one was marked with a red sun on the side. A bad feeling crept through Rosie.

The expression on the man's face showed he was up to nothing good, and when she looked up and around, more planes followed, the roars of their engines deafening.

"Rosie! Freddie! *Innerhalb!*" Mama called.

Freddie spread his arms and ran around the yard, mimicking the sounds made by the airplanes flying overhead. Rosie followed Freddie, flying across the yard with arms wide until a single thought fixed her into place, staring up into the sky. This wasn't a movie they were watching at the cinema. This—the planes, the smoke, the attack—was real.

Rosie looked toward the house and the panic on Mama's face infected her. Her breath caught and she froze in place until her mama's voice urging them inside broke through the roar of the planes.

"*Schnell Lieblinge! Im inneren!*" Mama called yet again.

"I'm the Army!" Freddie lowered his head and ran full speed toward Rosie. "You're the bomber!" He rammed into her and both fell to the ground.

"Gotcha!" Freddie scrambled to his feet and took off again.

Rosie stood slowly and scanned the sky, hoping to see the familiar Army planes chasing the menacing planes, but she saw only more of the same red suns winking down at them.

"Roselie! Frederick August! *Diese minute! Im hause!*" Mama called shrilly.

Rosie knew Mama meant it when she used their whole names *and* spoke in German. It was mostly in times of stress that Mama reverted to the old language.

Rosie caught her brother by the wrist and led him inside.

The radio blared. "This is the real McCoy! This is not a test! Pack food and clothing! Be prepared to evacuate to the hills. We are under attack by the Japs!" The announcer sounded like he was shouting to make sure everyone heard. "Pearl Harbor is under attack! Hawaii is under attack!"

"The real McCoy," Freddie said, zooming around the kitchen still in airplane mode. "The real McCoy! And that was a real Jap, Rosie. We saw a real Jap coming to drop bombs on us."

Drop bombs on *them*? The noise and the smoke. The planes were dropping bombs, but the explosions looked far away. Would they come back and drop bombs over their valley? Rosie, her knees weak with fear, had to sit down.

She looked up to see her mother leaning against the kitchen counter. Rosie needed to hear Mama say they were safe, that they would be okay. "Mama . . ." she started to say.

Mama straightened slowly and moved to the kitchen table. She placed her hand over Rosie's. Mama's hand felt cold and shook slightly. "Not to worry, *liebling*. He is not going to drop bombs on us!" she said quietly. "He will drop them on the Navy ships and the Army base, not on us."

Rosie took heart from Mama's brave words. Still, Mama was afraid. Rosie heard it in her voice. She put her arms around her mother's waist and hugged her tightly. Mama hugged her back. "We'll be all right," Rosie whispered. Mama nodded as she turned back to the sink.

Papa entered the kitchen quietly and took a seat across from Rosie. Together they listened to every word the announcer said. Rosie waited for Papa's added assurance that they would be safe, but he said nothing, an almost blank look on his face as if he couldn't believe what he was hearing.

Freddie had dug out one of his toy metal planes and flew it around the kitchen. Rosie wanted him to sit down, be quiet. But he was only seven and had no idea of the danger they were in.

"Papa, we could see the pilot's face," Rosie said. "He was flying so low. Why was he so low?" She couldn't stop thinking about the plane coming lower and lower, closer and closer.

"Ah, the valley makes a perfect path to the harbor. And the pilots dropped down to better hit their targets, I imagine," Papa answered, his voice shaky. His hands were clasped tightly as they rested on the table top, his knuckles white.

"But how did they fly all the way here from Japan?" Rosie asked.

"Not all the way, I would think. They probably flew from warships that brought them closer, close enough to attack." Papa rubbed his face.

"Why?" Rosie asked. "Why Hawaii?" People spoke always of their islands, the only home she'd ever known, as paradise, and she believed it wholeheartedly—the fair weather, the flowering plants, the friendly people, the land itself so welcoming to life. It was a sin to intrude on their paradise with bombs and . . . she tried to block the image but it came anyway: death.

"If the Japanese control Hawaii, they will control the Pacific. It will give them a base to attack both east and west." Papa shook his head. "But that will not happen." He took Rosie's hand and squeezed. "The Army will not let that happen . . . " his voice trailed off.

"But where are our planes? All the planes we saw were Japanese," Rosie said.

Papa shook his head and shrugged. Rosie noticed that his eyes glistened with tears.

Mama mumbled, "Not another war." She shook her head and repeated, "not another war."

"Do we need to pack? Be ready to go?" Rosie asked. "The man on the radio said be ready to evacuate." She felt an urgency to gather things she might need, that she couldn't live without—clothes, books, her journal, and food, of course.

Papa shook his head again. "That man is speaking his own fears of invasion. There is no official word."

"It will mean a war, Henry, another war." Papa stood and opened his arms. Mama leaned against his chest. "With the Germans. Last time we fought the Germans, it was terrible. People hated us."

"We have friends here, Greta. It will be different this time." He patted her back.

Rosie wasn't sure what her mama was talking about. Mama had lived in Hawaii during the last war, just like she did now—she'd never lived anyplace but Hawaii. Papa had been a young boy in Germany then and didn't like to talk about the war. He had come to America to study soon after and had never gone back. And now he was an American citizen like Mama, Rosie, and Freddie, who had been born here. He was so proud of his citizenship!

Rosie wondered if her Mama had been paying attention. "Mama, the war the Germans are fighting is in Europe." *And that is far, far away,* she thought as she spoke. "These are Japs doing the bombing. The radio said it was Japs."

"It will soon, very soon, be part of one big war," said Papa sadly. "And now it is here, too."

"But why . . ."

Papa interrupted. "There are some very bad men in charge. In Germany, Hitler; in Italy, Mussolini; in Japan, Tojo. They want to rule the world. Hitler has been stomping his way through Europe, conquering one country after another. So far, no one has been able to stop him. Maybe now we will have to be part of this war." Papa paused and shook his head. "*Liebes mädchen,* the world these men envision is not the world of America."

Conquer. "C-O-N-Q-U-E-R," Rosie spelled out loud, and then clapped her hand over her mouth. She'd started spelling words aloud ever since she'd become obsessed with winning the All-Hawaii spelling bee, especially when she was nervous. But how could she, in this moment of danger and uncertainty, even think about that silly spelling bee?

Papa's head pulled up sharply and a smile played at the corners of his mouth. "Ah, my spelling princess," he said. "Do you spell out your sentences before you speak them? Can you spell democracy?"

"D-E-M-O-C-R-A-C-Y," Rosie spelled easily.

"That is what we will be fighting for. Now, dictatorship, because that is what we are fighting against. That is how the Axis countries rule."

"D-I-C-T-A-T-O-R-S-H-I-P," Rosie spelled in a small voice. She had overheard Mama and Papa discussing Adolph Hitler and the Nazis in Germany, usually when they thought she and Freddie were asleep or busy elsewhere. Even though he hadn't seen them in many years, Papa had family in Germany and he worried about them.

The war in Europe had also been discussed in current events class at school, but it always seemed far away. Rosie had never expected war to show up practically in her front yard.

The radio had faded to static and Papa twirled the dial, trying to locate a station with a signal. "The bombs must have interfered with the towers, or perhaps the Army needs the radio frequency," Papa said as he stepped back and stared at the wooden box.

If Papa couldn't make the radio work, no one could. After all, Papa was the Radio King of the Hawaiian Islands. Everyone brought their broken sets to him to fix and relied on him to recommend the best set for their needs when they needed to buy a new radio.

Rosie knew he must feel lost without the radio telling him what was happening. She knew because she felt like a member of the family was missing without the words coming out of the air and into the house.

The sounds that took the place of those words—the whine of overhead planes and blasts of erratic explosions—added to the tension. Sirens had joined the din with a high-pitched up and down wail, and again she covered her ears.

Papa had leaned in close to the radio and was listening again. "They are saying to stay inside and stay off the roads," he said. "If you have medical training, you are needed to help with the wounded. They are bombing all the military installations—Pearl Harbor, Kanoehe Bay, Schofield Barracks, Hickam, everywhere."

Rosie pushed her chair back. She needed her journal. Perhaps if she wrote down what she saw and heard happening around her it would make her feel less frightened. And she would make a list of things to pack in case they did have to evacuate to the hills. She ran up the stairs to the family's living quarters and grabbed her journal and a pencil off her bed. As she turned to go back to the kitchen, she almost tripped over an orange ball of fur which rocketed out of the room and down the steps in front of her. Rosie tried to catch her cat but it shot out the kitchen door that someone—probably Freddie—had left ajar.

Chapter 2

"Kitty!" she called, thinking how scared her cat must be of all the loud noises and sirens.

Tossing the journal on the kitchen table, Rosie ran past her parents, ignoring their calls for her to stay inside. She slammed the screen door behind her.

The colorful flowering bushes along the edge of the property that divided their yard from that of the Tanakas was one of Kitty's favorite hiding spots. But Kitty wasn't there. Rosie ran down the hill to make sure the cat hadn't gone into the road.

She stopped short. There were no cars driving past their house. Rosie looked in both directions. Their absence added to the strangeness of this day.

The whine of planes overhead grew even louder as she searched for Kitty. She shaded her eyes and looked up. A group of Japanese planes was being chased by two American planes. Fire flew between the airplanes and suddenly one of the Japanese planes exploded and spiraled to the ground on the far side of the valley. A fire burned brightly at the crash site and Rosie watched and waited, hoping to see the pilot running from the inferno. How could someone survive such destruction? And how could the sailors and soldiers survive the bombs being dropped on them? She felt sick to her stomach. Her relief at seeing American planes was short-lived, as Japanese planes continued to stream overhead with no further sign of pursuit.

Papa grabbed her arm. "*Innerhalb!*" he said sharply and pulled her behind him.

"But Kitty ran out. I think she's scared," Rosie said. She had mixed feelings. She was frightened of the planes and the bombs they carried but she was equally frightened of losing her precious Kitty. Rosie was willing to fight her fear to save her pet.

Rosie caught a glimpse of their next-door neighbors, also shading their eyes as they looked toward the sky. "The Palus are outside," she continued, searching for her best friend, Leilani, among the family members gathered on the porch.

"That cat can take care of herself and so can the Palus," Papa said. He pulled Rosie inside, shut the back door firmly after them and clicked the lock, even though Rosie had never seen him or anyone in the family lock the door before. Surely he didn't believe it was that easy to keep out the Japs!

Time passed slowly as the sounds of explosions and the whine of planes faded. Only the sirens still blasted, their wavery tone providing a scary musical accompaniment to the hours spent waiting to see what would happen next.

As they waited for the all clear, Rosie stayed in her room and wrote in her journal about what was happening on their island—the dreadful sounds, the burning smells, and the face of the Japanese pilot she had seen flying overhead. *What does it mean to be in a war?* she wrote, her thoughts coming through the point of her pencil.

"Papa!" Rosie called out, dropping her pencil as a frightening thought occurred to her. Papa rushed into Rosie's room, pale faced. "What? Are you all right?"

Rosie swallowed hard, but her words still came out sounding strangled. "Papa, you won't have to be a soldier—you won't have to fight in this war, will you?"

Freddie leaned around Papa. "I want to be a soldier," he said, puffing out his chest.

"No, son, you don't, and at my age, no, I won't have to be a soldier. But we will all have to fight this war in some way, princess," Papa answered.

Rosie picked up her journal and followed Papa to the living room, thinking about what her father had just said.

She sat down and wrote: *It's time for Papa to stop calling me princess. How can he call me "princess" and say we have to fight a war in the same sentence? It doesn't follow. He might be the radio king, but it doesn't automatically make me a princess. Now how do I tell him?*

Sunday afternoons usually meant a trip to the beach, an aloha day, as Rosie had called it since she was a little girl. The neighboring Palu brothers would sometimes give her, their younger sister Leilani, and Freddie a surfing lesson while Auntie Palu, their mother, gave Mama a quilting lesson. Papa and Uncle Palu usually stared at the sea and smoked, doing what Papa called "thinking about the path of life." Rosie had no idea what that meant, but as she looked at Papa's worried face staring out the window, she thought it was not a good path their lives were suddenly taking.

Mama broke the silence by asking Rosie to fill milk bottles with water, "just in case." Rosie hurried down the stairs to the kitchen, glad to have something to do. When she heard the knock on the door, she flung it open without a thought just as Papa called out for her to wait and let him answer it.

"Helloooo my nearest and dearest neighbor," Auntie Palu greeted Rosie as she stepped inside the house. Leilani stood behind her mother, arms crossed and frowning.

"Auntie Palu! Leilani!" Rosie answered. The woman was dressed in her normal brightly colored muumuu. The dress and Auntie's smile brightened the room, which had taken on the gloom of the overhanging smoke clouds. Leilani held back, remaining silent, which gave Rosie a prick of worry. Before she could ask what the matter was, Auntie Palu spoke again.

"Where is your mama? Is everyone here all right? I brought you a bowl of haupia. I know it is your favorite," she said in her singsong voice.

Rosie took the wooden bowl the woman held out and stood back as her neighbor walked past, calling for Mama.

"Auntie!" Mama said from midway down the stairs. Papa stood directly above her. "You startled us!"

"Ah, you think maybe the Japs will knock on the door before they come inside?" Auntie Palu laughed loudly.

"We weren't expecting anyone on such a day," Mama replied, her cheeks turning pink.

"But we must go on," Auntie said. "My boys, they go to the town to see what is happening there, and me, I don't want to think about it. Come, let us quilt and let our spirit animals lead us to peace."

Mama and Papa looked at each other as Auntie Palu joined them on the stairs, and then stepped aside as she led the way to the second-floor living room.

Leilani remained in the doorway, staring at the floor, refusing to meet Rosie's eyes.

"Are you all right?" Rosie asked, concerned. "Are you worried about your brothers?"

"I'm fine," Leilani said abruptly as she finally made her way up the stairs.

Rosie quickly set the creamy coconut pudding in the refrigerator and hurried to join everyone upstairs.

Leilani stood away from the adults, staring out the window.

Rosie joined her. "Want to go to my room?"

Leilani shook her head.

Rosie grew more worried. What was the matter with her friend? "We could look at the list of spelling words George brought me." Her aunt's boyfriend worked for the newspaper that sponsored the All-Hawaii spelling bee, and he had brought her a copy of the official guide book.

"You mean your cheat sheet?" Leilani said.

"It's not cheating! Anyone who wants to go pick up the guide at the newspaper can have one," Rosie said quickly.

"But, you are the only one who does have one," Leilani said.

"But . . . but . . . we both won." Rosie was at a loss. The two of them were declared co-champions when they exhausted the list of words provided by the spelling bee organizers. They both would proceed to the All-Island round.

"Did we?" Leilani grabbed a newspaper lying on the floor. She folded it open and held it in front of Rosie.

"Yes! I forgot to show you this," Auntie Palu said, grabbing the newspaper before Rosie had a chance to see what Leilani was trying to show her. She spread it so Mama and Papa could see.

"Isn't that lovely?" Mama said, smiling at Rosie.

"You look like a princess," said Papa.

Papa and his princesses! Rosie was tired of hearing it but she still couldn't bring herself to ask Papa to stop.

Rosie leaned over Auntie's shoulder. The headline read: CAN YOU SPELL W-I-N-N-E-R-S?" And Rosie remembered that a photographer had caught her in the library after school when she was returning books. She had taken Rosie's picture and asked her a few questions, but she hadn't said anything about publishing it in the newspaper. And why didn't they take Leilani's picture? There were pictures of winners from all over Oahu. Then Rosie remembered. Leilani had left early on Friday because she had a headache. If only she and Papa had looked at the rest of the paper instead of just the funnies, she would have seen the photo of only herself.

"That happened on Friday after you left school," Rosie said, "and look, it says, 'Not Pictured: Leilani Palu, who will also be competing in the finals.'"

Rosie imagined how slighted Leilani must feel. She had been so proud of winning the spelling bee because she had always excelled in sports but not in schoolwork. After all, she had to compete with big brothers.

"Who is going to read that small print? And, when did you decide to go to Punahou School next year? You haven't mentioned that to me!" Leilani blinked rapidly and a tear rolled slowly down one cheek.

"I'm sorry! I'm so sorry, but the Punahou thing," Rosie looked to Mama for help, "that just happened. We visited one weekend and they *invited* me to apply. I don't know if I'm going or not. I still have to be accepted. I didn't want to say anything until I knew something for sure."

Mama had given a talk about storytelling to the teachers at Punahou School and Rosie had tagged along. After the talk, one of the teachers had offered to give them a tour of the private academy. Rosie knew as soon as she'd seen all the school had to offer that it was the place for her.

"You will be," Leilani said, "after all, your family is *Kamaaina*."

"Leilani, you should not take that tone with your friend!" Auntie Palu broke in. "And Rosie may be part of a well-known, respected family in the islands, but your family has been here even longer. I told you, both of you would be welcome at Punahou."

"I doubt it," Leilani said under her breath.

Rosie wondered how she could make things right with her friend. She tried again. "I have some books for you," Rosie said to Leilani. "Nancy Drew!"

"You girls and your mysteries!" Auntie Palu said with a laugh. "You may want to take a few pointers from that detective girl and keep your eyes open for spies and saboteurs right here in Hawaii."

Before she could even think of what she was saying, the letters burst out of Rosie, "S-A-B-O-T-E-U-R."

"See, Mama, I told you. She . . . she . . . she thinks she knows everything," Leilani burst out and ran down the stairs.

Rosie heard the door slam.

For once, Auntie seemed speechless. Her mouth opened and shut. She pressed her lips together.

"Auntie, I'm so sorry. I didn't know about the picture. I'm sorry." Rosie blinked back tears.

Auntie Palu put her arm around Rosie. "This will pass. It has been a very bad day. Leilani was upset about the photo before the bombs started falling, then her brothers went away saying they were going after Japs. I think she is all mixed up. Be patient, lovey," Auntie said, "save yourself for the big battles."

Then Auntie dropped her own bombshell. "And as far as the spelling bee goes, no school for a while, meaning no spelling contest."

"What?" Rosie pulled away from Auntie. She turned to Mama. "But my papers for Punahou! The recommendations, the grades, they are due with my application next *Wednesday*!"

"*Liebling*, no school. Punahou will be closed as well," Mama assured her.

Hope sparked. "You think? You sure?"

Mama nodded.

But still, no school? Rosie had been wondering how her other friends—Mollie, Norma, Veronica—and their families had fared during the bombing. Norma and Veronica both had dads who were in the military. Many of the kids in her class had family in the armed services. And Rosie knew, from the number of bombs dropped and the explosions she had seen firsthand, that people had died. And here she was worrying about a spelling contest and a school application.

"And Mama, what about the *kinder?*" Rosie asked. "Will we open for them?" Her mother ran a kindergarten on the first floor of their home during the week for young children whose parents worked.

"We'll have to see if businesses are open, if the *mutters* and *vaters* need us," Mama said with a shrug.

Auntie picked a different newspaper out of the basket she had brought along and opened to another story. "No school and no lights! How can we read? How can we sew? How can we even cook with no lights?"

"It will all need to be done before dark. Or the windows will need to be covered," Papa said.

"Blackout, hmph!" Auntie continued. "They found us once. They will find us again."

The room grew quiet. Rosie tried not to think about the possibility of . . . again. No matter what Mama had said, next time they might not bomb just the ships and planes and soldiers.

"Speaking of the blackout, I think it will soon turn dark. Shall I walk you home?" Papa asked Auntie, standing up.

Auntie Palu looked at him, surprised. "No," she said. "I am capable of making my own way." She carefully folded her very complicated and beautiful blue and white quilt square and put it back in her sewing basket. "And I should check on Leilani."

"Thank you," Mama said. "I needed a good dose of you to clear my mind." She hugged Auntie. Rosie lined up to give her own hug to the woman and Freddie followed suit. The newspaper remained, crumpled, on the floor by the chair where Auntie had dropped it.

"I need a surfing lesson," said Freddie, holding on to Auntie's middle.

"Next Sunday, dear one," she replied, then in a whisper added, "next Sunday."

As soon as she heard the door shut, Rosie picked up the newspaper that lay where Auntie had dropped it. 3RD EXTRA the masthead proclaimed. That must mean there were two earlier extra editions printed before this one. She wished she could see them, too, but this would have to do. She skimmed the headlines:

MARTIAL LAW DECLARED;

DEATHS ARE MOUNTING

OVER 400 KILLED HERE;

JAPAN ANNOUNCES "WAR"

Japanese Raids On Guam, Panama Are Reported

Oahu Blackout Tonight; Fleet Here Moves Out to Sea

As Rosie skimmed through the paper, she read that some civilians, in addition to military, had been wounded or killed by both bombs and machine gun fire. While she and Freddie had fooled around outside like little kids, they'd been in more danger than she had imagined.

"Rosie, what are you doing?" Mama asked, looking up from her quilting.

"Reading the paper," Rosie said from behind the pages.

Papa took the paper out of her hands and folded it closed. "You do not need to read all that bad news."

"Please," she said. "I want to know what's happening."

Papa shook his head and stuck the paper between the cushions of his chair. "All you need to know is no school tomorrow and no lights on tonight."

"But . . ."

"No more newspaper. It's enough to give you nightmares. It's enough to give me nightmares." Papa stared out the window beside his chair. "Go help your mama with dinner."

The last thing Rosie cared to think about was food, but standing beside Mama in the kitchen, setting the table, and joining her singing some of the silly songs Mama sang with the little ones did make her feel better. When Freddie came in and joined them, making up his own song about a little airplane instead of a little teapot—"Here is my nose cone, here are my wings," she and Mama laughed. Rosie thought it was the first time since she had read the funnies with Papa before the bombing started, many hours ago, that she had anything to laugh about.

Chapter 3

Light faded quickly as they ate dinner. Papa kept reminding them that they would have to spend the evening in the dark and to do what needed to be done while they could still see.

Rosie didn't know what they would do except go to bed if the house had to be dark. They couldn't even listen to their regular radio programs because the stations were still static.

Before she went upstairs to bed, Rosie checked outside to see if Kitty had returned. The cat sat on the top step of the porch and when the door opened, ran upstairs. Rosie followed Kitty straight to her bedroom where the cat crawled under the covers.

As Rosie dressed for bed, she found the quiet disturbing. The streets were *too* quiet after the noise of the day, especially with no cars driving by, and the neighborhood was darker than she'd ever seen it. The newspaper, the little she had read, had reported that any visible sliver of light would be immediately shot out. Rosie listened, but heard nothing that sounded like gunfire. Everyone must be following directions.

When Mama and Papa came in to say good night, Rosie asked, "May I sleep under the Queen's quilt?" Only on special occasions did Mama allow the first quilt she'd ever made to come down from its place of honor on the wall. Rosie loved that quilt: it told the story of their family in fabric, each piece like the page of a book sewn together in what Auntie called a crazy quilt, different than Hawaiian style. Mama had designed it after she'd viewed one similar on a trip to Iolani Palace, where the kings and queens of Hawaii had lived in Honolulu. That one was sewn by Queen Liliuokalani, the last ruler of Hawaii, and its squares told the story of the islands in the years before they became a US territory. It, too, was called the Queen's quilt.

Mama and Papa exchanged looks and Mama finally nodded. Papa disappeared for a moment and came back with the quilt gathered in his arms. When he dropped it over her, Rosie smelled the roses of Mama's perfume. "And tell me the story," she said, pulling it tightly about her.

"Mama! Mama! Who is going to read to me? I can't sleep if you don't read to me," Freddie yelled from his room.

Rosie stiffened as Mama and Papa both turned toward the hallway. She didn't want them to leave her alone in the dense darkness. Papa held a flashlight pointed to the floor and that provided a comforting glimmer of light.

"I'll go, although how I will read a story in this dark is a mystery to me," Mama said.

Papa sat on the edge of Rosie's bed, and she let herself sink back into the pillows.

Mama gave Papa a quick kiss on the top of his balding head and headed toward Freddie's room. Before she reached the doorway, she turned and came back, staring down at Rosie. "I love you, coconut." She gave Rosie a kiss as well.

"Me, too," Rosie said.

"Try to sleep, *liebling*. You may need your rest, for tomorrow will be a different day," Mama said.

No school for one thing, thought Rosie, *war for another.* She shivered and drew the quilt more tightly around her.

"Okay, Papa, start at the beginning, when Mama's family came to Hawaii."

"The sugar business on Kauai . . ." Papa began.

"I love Kauai," Rosie said. "Do you think the war is there yet? It's not that far from Oahu."

"I hope not. I don't know why the Japanese would want to bomb sugar plantations. Everyone loves sugar! They probably flew right over it," Papa said.

"So," he continued, "the Rauschling family came to Kauai to work on a sugar plantation at the invitation of Sugar King Spreckels himself."

Rosie fingered the embroidery depicting a stand of sugar cane against the eight Hawaiian islands.

"And your mama was born right there in the middle of a sugar cane . . ." Papa paused and grinned at Rosie.

"You are teasing. She was not born in a field." Rosie had heard the story many times and Papa always made the same joke.

"Ah, I did not say field. A sugar cane plantation in the US territory of Hawaii, making her a citizen of that great country from the day she was born."

Rosie moved to the next square, which featured an embroidered outline of Germany. "And your family was still in the old country, making radios."

Papa nodded. "I came to the United States to learn to make even better radios and before I leave, I travel to the islands and meet your beautiful mama who was engaged to be married to a sugar prince."

"Who was engaged to Aunt Yvonne before Mama caught his eye."

"That is correct. I am glad I in turn caught your Mama's eye and she chose me over the sugar prince," Papa said.

"And when you and Mama married, no one was happy about that, right?"

"Mama and I were very happy but my family disowned me because I would not return to Germany. And her family told us we were not welcome on the plantation on Kauai because your mama, she broke both your Aunt Yvonne's and the sugar prince's heart.

"So, we moved to Oahu, to Honolulu, the biggest city in all of Hawaii, and we open our own business, a radio business."

Rosie touched the picture of the radio sewn on the quilt. "And then I was born."

"A radio princess," Papa said, stroking Rosie's hair.

"That was when I was little," Rosie said. "Maybe I'm too old to be a princess now."

"Maybe you think you should be queen?" asked Papa.

"No, not queen either. I don't want to be a princess just because you are the king. I want to be something . . . well, something that I earned."

"What shall that be?" Papa asked.

"I'm still deciding," Rosie said.

"Is Freddie still the radio prince?" Papa asked.

"Until he decides to be something else," Rosie said.

"So then the radio prince came along," Papa said and he continued to tell the story of buying a small house near Diamond Head on the east side of the island, then moving to their present house across the island on the west side of Honolulu after Mama decided to buy a kindergarten and be the teacher she had always dreamed of being. "The sugar prince had never approved of that wish of your mama's," he added.

"Now Mama will have to make a war square," said Rosie sadly.

"Ah, *liebling*." Papa gathered her into his arms and held her close.

Mama returned and stood in the doorway. Papa kissed Rosie one last time and joined Mama, putting his arm around her shoulders as they walked away.

As soon as they were out of sight, she scooted Kitty out from under the covers and the cat curled herself against Rosie's chest. She tried to take comfort from Kitty's warmth and purrs, but it was hard to fall asleep. Normally, she would have read as long as she could stay awake, but with no light that bedtime ritual was out. She wished she could write in her journal, but it was too dark. Or was it? There was a moon, though not a full bright one.

Rosie carried her journal to the window and lifted the shade a tiny bit, adjusting the pages in the sliver of light that entered from outside. She wrote:

Leilani is angry with me and I don't know why. There's no one I would rather be up against in the spelling bee because I will be happy if either of us wins. Of course if I win, I will be a champion, or as Papa would say, the "Princess of Spelling." It will look very good on my application to Punahou. How can Leilani think me going to Punahou will change anything? I will still live next door to her. I hope Auntie is right and Leilani has confused her feelings about the war with her feelings about the spelling bee.

And the war. Mama says it will be different days. I suppose so, but as long as we are together I think we will be all right.

Chapter 4

Rosie lay in bed squinting against the bright sunlight. It was such a contrast to last night, when she finally fell asleep in deepest darkness. Slowly, she sat up. She patted the warm spot beside her—Kitty was gone, but not long ago. Rosie stretched and yawned, then slid off her bed. For only a moment, she wondered why Mama hadn't awakened her for school. Then she remembered. The War.

Rosie quickly dressed in the pink and blue flowered dress she'd worn to school Friday that was still lying across the desk chair. No school, so no need to bother with shoes.

In the kitchen, Rosie found four of Mama's *kinder* sitting around the table, each with a fried egg and a glass of pineapple juice. Different. Mama considered the kitchen part of their home and it was usually off limits to the kids.

"It's cozier in here," Mama answered, before Rosie could

even ask about the change in routine. "And, none of the teachers have shown up yet so I will need your help today."

Rosie loved to help out with the *kinder*. Her usual job at the kindergarten involved lots of soap and water and cleaning. A chance to work with the *kinder* was a treat!

Rosie had planned to visit the Palus but that would have to wait if Mama needed her. She wanted, as soon as possible, to see if she could straighten out what Leilani had clearly misunderstood.

"Hi, Rosie," said a small voice. It was Chester. For some reason she could not understand, he had attached himself to her from his first day at the kindergarten. He tagged after her like Kitty sometimes did, but unlike Kitty, he talked the entire time. "I like eggs. Do you like eggs? Did you hear the bombs yesterday? My mom is a nurse so she has been at the hospital all night long. She brought me here so she could go to sleep . . ."

"Hi, Chester," Rosie said, "I'm glad you're here. We'll talk in a minute."

"Promise?" said Chester.

Rosie nodded as she turned to ask Mama, "Where's Papa?"

Chester answered first. "Your daddy was backing out of the driveway when we drove up and he almost hit my mom's car. She said if we wrecked our car now, we wouldn't get another one until the war was over. Did you know that, Rosie? We won't be able to get a new car because I guess the Japs bombed all the new cars."

Chester loved cars, Rosie knew, so this would be a very bad thing in his world. As usual, he had a toy car parked beside his plate. Still, she needed to talk to Mama. She held up her hand, "Later, remember? Promise."

Chester nodded and ate more of his egg.

"He went into the store. He was very worried about damage. And he expects some business today. People will want to have a radio to hear what is happening."

Rosie certainly understood that. Yet, the radio wasn't turned on in their kitchen. She looked at it sitting silently on the small table near the doorway.

"I don't want to frighten the *kinder*," Mama said, again answering Rosie's question before she could ask. "And the reception is still only now and then."

"Hello? Is anyone home?" Malia, one of Mama's teachers, stepped in the back door. "You have children here!" she said, looking surprised.

"But no teachers," Mama said, "so I'm glad you made it."

"I called the other teachers and told them no need to come in today," Malia said.

"You did what?" Mama said, turning to face the older Hawaiian woman.

Uh-oh, thought Rosie. Malia had owned the kindergarten—or nursery as she had called it—before Mama. Mama had kept her on as a teacher, but Malia sometimes forgot she wasn't in charge any longer, according to conversations Rosie had overheard between Mama and Papa.

"Malia, that is not your place," Mama said sharply. "But what is done is done. We have a small group today, and Rosie is here to help out so we will manage, but . . ."

"You would think the parents would want to be with their *keiki*, their children, on a day like today," Malia interrupted, "not drop them off for others to care for. At least that is the way we Hawaiians feel . . ."

"I am sure our parents would prefer to stay home today but some of them have jobs that make that impossible. The nurses and hospital workers, for instance," said Mama, turning away from Malia. "It's not our place to judge. Will you please lead the children in circle time?"

"Yes, boss, that I will." Malia glared at Mama's back before gathering the little ones and marching them into the classroom.

"Rosie, what do you want for breakfast?" Mama asked.

"I'm okay," she replied. "What do you need me to do?"

"First, let me braid that hair of yours." Mama smiled at her, but Rosie could tell it was forced.

She ran upstairs and grabbed her hairbrush. Chester met her halfway down the staircase and grabbed her hand.

"You need to go to the classroom with the rest of the kids," Rosie said, pointing the way.

"I told Auntie Malia I had to go to the bathroom. I want you to come be our teacher."

"I will be there in a minute," Rosie said, making another promise.

"We're in a war," Chester said. "Did you know that, Rosie? We are fighting the Japs now and pretty soon we'll be fighting the Nazis, too. Is your dad a Nazi?"

"Nazi? What do you mean?" Rosie asked, surprised to hear "Nazi"—a word she hated—coming out of such a little mouth.

"Mommy said your mom and dad might be Nazis and she wasn't sure she should leave me here . . ."

"Mama and Papa are not Nazis!" Rosie said hotly. The word brought to mind pictures of men in black uniforms marching in perfect step. Adolph Hitler and his stupid black mustache. A red and white flag with what looked like a spider in the center. All running through her mind like the news-reels she'd seen at the movies.

Chester dropped her hand, his head hanging. "But they might be," he whispered.

Rosie struggled to keep the anger she felt out of her voice. Chester couldn't have any idea what he was saying. He was a little kid, repeating what he had heard. And to learn that he had heard people suspected her mama and papa of being Nazis was shocking!

"Downstairs! Find Malia," Rosie said. She waited for him to go, feeling slightly sick to her stomach.

In the kitchen Mama motioned for Rosie to sit in a chair without a word. Mama looked so tired and sad, Rosie couldn't tell her what Chester had said. She tried to relax in the silence as Mama brushed her hair in slow, gentle strokes. For a moment, life felt normal as Mama braided Rosie's long, dark hair. Mama kissed her on top of her head and patted her shoulder. "Please, help Malia."

In the classroom, Malia had the children, three boys and one girl, sitting at a table with crayons and paper. Every one of the children was drawing an airplane. Some of the planes had red fire around them, others were surrounded by gray shapes, what Rosie suspected was smoke.

"Rosie is not a Nazi," Chester said to Malia, breaking the silence.

Malia shrugged. "Time will tell," she said, not looking at Rosie.

What did she mean by that? The Nazi talk added to Rosie's sense of unease. She busied herself choosing a story to read to the children. A happy story with no planes and no war.

"Hey, guys!" Freddie leaned in the door that led from the classroom to the play yard. "Come on out here! Want to play war?"

"Freddie, do you really think . . ." Rosie started to say as the boys pushed back their chairs and rushed to join her brother. Susi stayed behind and laid her head on the table.

"Should we let them do that?" Rosie asked Malia.

She nodded. "As your mother would tell us in her *haole* words, it's their way of working through their fears," Malia said.

Chester leaned back inside the screen door. "Susi is a Jap. C'mon, Susi. Try to bomb us again, you dirty Jap! We will chase you in our airplanes and shoot you down!" he yelled at her.

"I don't want to be a dirty Jap," Susi said, bursting into tears.

Malia stood aside and watched the little girl sob.

Rosie realized that Susi was the only one of their Japanese students who had come to school that day. The boys were all *haole*, white. When she thought of how many of their neighbors were Japanese, Rosie felt a twinge of fear, especially when she remembered the expression on the face of the Jap flying the bomber right above her head yesterday. What if the Japanese on the islands decided to turn on the *haoles*?

Stop scaring yourself over nothing, Rosie warned herself. It wasn't the Japanese who lived in Hawaii who had bombed the island. They were no doubt as troubled over the war as the *haoles*, more troubled probably because they looked like the pilots who had bombed them.

When Malia still didn't move to help the little girl, Rosie knelt beside her. "What would you like to play, Susi?"

"I want," she said, taking a breath. "I want to take a nap."

Rosie looked up at Malia who shrugged again and turned away.

"Let's fix you a cot, then." Rosie took one of the napping cots off the stack and went to Susi's cubby and found her blanket and a small Japanese doll. Susi was already curled up on the cot by the time Rosie returned. She tucked the blanket around the girl and handed her the doll. Susi stuck her thumb in her mouth and closed her eyes.

"Will you be in here to watch her if I go check on the boys?" Rosie asked Malia.

Malia had settled herself in a grown-up-sized chair. "You go ahead. Those little rascals are bound to be in trouble soon."

Led by Freddie, the boys were all pretending to be airplanes. He had even managed to find a scarf that he had wrapped around his neck, like the pilot they had seen the day before.

Rosie turned away from the boys when she heard a car crunching up the drive. A large black car pulled to a stop by the back door. Rosie didn't recognize either the car or the men dressed in dark suits and wearing gray fedoras who stepped out of it.

"We'd like to speak to Mr. or Mrs. Schatzer," the taller of the two men said in a gruff voice.

"My father is at work," Rosie said quickly, "but Mama, she's in the kitchen. Let me show you the way." Over her shoulder, she yelled at her brother, "Hey, watch the kids."

All of the boys had stopped their battle and stared silently at the men, looking between them and the car.

Rosie's braids bounced against her back as she led the two men to the back door. "Mama?" she called through the screen. "There are some men here . . ."

The taller man gently moved Rosie to the side and opened the screen. "Mrs. Schatzer," he said as he flipped open what looked like his wallet and held it out to Mama.

"Is it Henry? Is something wrong with . . ."

"No, ma'am," the man said quickly. "We'd like you to come with us and answer a few questions. Where is Mr. Schatzer?"

"He's—he's at work," Mama said, patting her hair. "Come with you? Where? I have the children . . ."

"It's not a request. You will come with me, now."

"May I please gather my sweater and purse? Put on some lipstick and brush my hair?" She untied her apron and hung it over the back of the chair.

"Mama," Rosie reached out, panic taking hold of her.

"It's okay, *liebling*," Mama said, her face as pale as Rosie had ever seen it. "I will be back before dinner. And Malia is here."

The tall man held open the screen door.

"Just a moment," Mama said, heading toward the stairs. The man followed closely behind her, and Rosie gasped as his coat flipped open and she saw he had a gun resting snugly in a holster under his arm. Why did he need a gun? Was it because of the war? Who was he?

The second man stayed behind, standing in front of the door with his arms folded across his chest.

Rosie took a few steps toward the staircase intending to follow Mama, but she didn't want to leave the second man in the kitchen alone. She kept her eyes on the stairs and strained to hear anything Mama or the man might say to give her a clue who the men were and where they were taking her mother. She heard nothing but footsteps.

In minutes Mama reappeared, her hair straightened, her

lipstick shining, wearing a soft blue sweater and carrying her purse across her arm.

"Let me tell my teacher what is happening," Mama said, heading toward the classroom, but the man who was staying close behind her grabbed her arm and stopped her.

"Let her tell her," he said, pointing at Rosie. "We need to go now."

Mama's shoulders slumped as she let the man lead her to the car.

"Mama, where are you going? When will you be back?" Rosie called from the porch, her stomach feeling like it was turning inside out.

Her mother smiled weakly. "Don't worry. I will be with Papa and we will be home by suppertime. Tell Malia to call parents to pick up their children and ask her to please stay . . ."

The man pushed Mama into the back seat of the car and slammed the door. He touched the brim of his hat and nodded toward Rosie.

"Mama!" she called again, fighting tears. Why was her mother leaving her there? Where were they taking her? Rosie watched her mama turn and look out the back window at her, waving.

Chapter 5

Rosie pressed the palms of her hands against her eyes to keep from crying. She repeated to herself over and over, *Mama will be home before supper, she will be home before supper.*

"Mrs. Schatzer!" Rosie heard Malia call.

"She's gone," Rosie said weakly through the screen door.

Malia opened the door, looking puzzled. "But we have children to care for," she said.

"Some men came, in suits and a big black car, and they wanted to ask her questions. And she said she will be back before supper. And for you to call the parents to come pick up the kids and would you please stay with us until she gets back." Rosie said everything as fast as she could before her voice broke, hoping she remembered it all. She waited for Malia to say something to reassure her.

"Government men?" Malia said, almost as if she was talking to herself. "They arrested Mrs. Schatzer?"

Government men? Why would Malia think the men were from the government?

"No! Why would anyone want to arrest my mama? They only want to ask her questions," Rosie said quickly. "They went someplace to talk. You know how it is here with all the kids around." But she swallowed hard, remembering the gun. Did that man *arrest* her mama? Why? Why? Had they accidentally broken one of the new war rules that had popped up seemingly in an instant?

Malia stared pointedly at Rosie, her hands on her hips. She said nothing, only shook her head as she walked slowly toward Mama's office.

Rosie hesitated a moment, not sure what to do with herself, wanting Malia to tell her. She followed her into the office and the teacher was already on the phone. Malia turned her back and lowered her voice, talking the pidgin of the islands.

Rosie knew her mother would want Malia to make sure the *kinder* were cared for before anything else and she suspected Malia wasn't talking to parents. Still Rosie held back. She knew Malia wouldn't like a girl telling her what to do. She didn't even like Mama telling her what to do! Rosie wondered if this was one of the battles Papa had mentioned they would have to fight in these different days. She took a breath. "Shouldn't you be calling parents?" she asked. Her voice didn't sound one bit like that of a fighter. It sounded more like that of a squeaky mouse. Rosie waited, dreading what might come next.

Malia glared at her, spoke a few more words Rosie couldn't hear, then hung up the phone. The teacher sat at Mama's desk and pulled out the list of parents' names, addresses, and phone numbers.

Rosie breathed deeply. She'd done it.

In the kitchen, Rosie sat at the table. Should she call Papa when Malia finished the calls to parents?

Before she could decide, Malia appeared and announced, "The parents are coming."

"Thanks." Rosie didn't know what else to say. She stood as Malia took a seat at the kitchen table.

"I'm going to call my father," Rosie said, picking up the kitchen phone. The line sputtered with intermittent static as the operator asked for the number in a harried voice. The phone at Papa's shop rang and rang and rang. To her ears, it echoed as though it was ringing in an empty room.

"There is no answer at that number," the operator said.

"Please try again," Rosie asked.

Again, no answer.

"Papa must be on his way home," she said to Malia, hoping it was true.

Malia only stared, smiling slightly in a way that made Rosie feel she knew more than she was telling.

Before Rosie could confront her, three parents arrived at almost the same time—but not Chester's. Susi Ogura's mother carried her to the car, still asleep. Malia refused to talk to her, mumbling under her breath about "tricky Japs."

Rosie was extra friendly and nice to Mrs. Ogura, talking louder than necessary to make sure she didn't hear Malia's mumbles, although Susi's mother's quick exit made Rosie think she wasn't fooling her at all. The parents of the two boys barely said a word to either the teacher or Rosie, but hurried the boys into their cars as if they feared their child was in danger.

What had Malia told them when she called? Rosie figured it wasn't anything good—and maybe not even true.

"Where did Mama go?" Freddie asked, when only he and Chester were left.

"She'll be back soon," Rosie said, hoping Malia wouldn't say anything about her thought that Mama had been arrested. Maybe Mama would return before Freddie demanded an answer.

"School is boring today," Chester said.

Before Rosie could come up with suggestions for play, the screen door slammed. Was Mama home? She rushed to the kitchen.

A noisy green pickup truck idled beside the porch and Malia was climbing into it.

Rosie ran outside. "Malia! Where are you going?"

"Bye-bye," Malia said as the driver backed down the driveway.

"There are still kids here! And you're supposed to stay until Mama comes back!" Rosie yelled at the disappearing vehicle.

Rosie wrapped her arms around herself as tightly as she could. Like it or not, she was in charge. Mama had left her alone with Freddie before, but never alone with the *kinder*.

"Hey! I'm hungry!" Chester leaned out the door.

Rosie felt the comforting softness of Kitty curling herself around her ankles.

"Kitty! There's Kitty!" Chester yelled, slamming the door and running toward them.

Immediately, Kitty took off for the thicket at the back of the property.

Rosie sighed. She was in charge, so she'd better take charge. "Pancakes!" she said. "How does that sound?"

"I love pancakes!" Chester said. "And I can help. I always help my mom."

Good thing he likes pancakes, Rosie thought, *since it is the only thing I know how to cook*. Besides soup. And soup was what Mama would fix to make her feel better when she was feeling down. It didn't work when Mama was the *reason* she felt down.

They had finished the pancakes and Freddie was clearing the table with Chester's help when Chester's mother arrived, dark rings around her eyes. "Where's Mrs. Schatzer?" she demanded.

"She isn't here right now," Rosie admitted.

"Then let me talk to another teacher."

Rosie shook her head. Chester's mother was not happy.

"You! You have been taking care of my child?"

"Only for a little while. And I watch my brother all the time. Really, I'm very responsible," Rosie tried to assure her.

"I hope your mother doesn't expect me to pay for this." She grabbed her son's hand and pulled him toward the door.

"We played war, Mommy. And I won! I was the Army. Rosie was a Nazi . . ."

"Played war? You are living a war." The mother looked over her shoulder at Rosie. "And as far as playing a Nazi goes, well . . ." She tossed her head and marched out the door.

Chapter 6

What now? Rosie thought. Papa hadn't answered the phone, but what about the rest of her family? Should she call one of Mama's sisters, Tante Etta or Tante Yvonne?

Her family would surely want to know what had happened to Mama, wouldn't they? Especially Tante Etta, who had lived with them when she attended university on Oahu. She was much younger than Mama and like a big sister to Rosie and Freddie. Or maybe Rosie should wait, and give Mama a chance to return. It was still early in the afternoon.

Slowly, Rosie trudged up the stairs and picked up her journal, then found the book she'd been reading. Her spelling list lay open on her desk, so she grabbed that as well. Rosie carried them all into the living room and curled up in Papa's chair.

Usually Rosie had no trouble disappearing into her Nancy Drew books, but today every time a car drove by—although they were few and far between—she jumped up to see if it was Mama returning. She didn't even feel like writing in her journal. There was almost too much to write about. She doodled pictures on the empty page—an airplane, an American flag, a star.

Freddie had spread his Lincoln logs throughout the room, building an Army base.

Rosie brought in the radio from the kitchen and twirled the dial, trying to find a station. When she heard a familiar voice, she stopped and adjusted the dial. The president, Mr. Roosevelt, was speaking.

Freddie moved closer to the radio, listening.

"Yesterday, December 7, 1941—a date which will live in infamy," he said.

I-N-F-A-M-Y, Rosie spelled silently as Freddie leaned his head against her leg and they listened as President Roosevelt spoke.

Rosie heard how the Japanese also attacked Hong Kong, Guam, the Philippine Islands, Wake Island, and Midway Island. *Other islands are also right in the middle of the war,* she thought, taking a strange comfort from the thought that Hawaii wasn't the only target.

The president admitted that they were in danger, and Freddie squeezed into the chair beside her. Roosevelt's final words asked the Congress to declare war. But Rosie—and the rest of Hawaii—knew the war had already begun.

When the speech ended, the announcer said it had been given earlier in the day by the President and would be repeated, then static filled the air again. Rosie turned off the radio with a sigh. What she really wanted to hear was music—happy snappy music.

"I want Mama," Freddie said.

"Soon," Rosie said, hoping she was right. Freddie's words were painful, echoing her own wish. "Find something to play," she said.

"But . . ."

"Play," she said firmly.

Her brother picked up a Lincoln log and turned it over and over.

Rosie opened her journal and wrote:

"Yesterday, December 7, 1941—a date which will live in infamy—the United States of America was suddenly and deliber-ately attacked by naval and air forces of the Empire of Japan." This is what President Roosevelt called the day of the bombing, "a date which will live in infamy." And then he asked Congress to declare war. War. Against the Japs and the Germans and the Italians. I'm not glad we were bombed, but I am glad it was Japan that did it and not Germany. After all, Papa is from Germany even though he is an American now. And Chester already called us Nazis. And he is a baby!

Something tugged at the back of Rosie's mind. If Chester attached that label to them, what might others think? But, perhaps the government needed Mama to help translate German! They didn't think she was a Nazi!

T-R-A-N-S-L-A-T-E, she spelled. Yes, that could be it. And as soon as she had a chance Mama would call. Rosie relaxed slightly.

"Should I call Tante Yvonne?" she finally asked Freddie, the two of them still sharing the chair, although Freddie had started to squirm.

"Or maybe Tante Etta?" he said.

Rosie nodded and headed for the phone. She picked up the receiver. Instead of a buzz or the sound of the operator asking what number she wanted, Rosie heard only silence on the line. She jiggled the buttons a few times, but still there was silence. So, no Mama, no Papa, no telephone.

"The phone isn't working," Rosie told her brother.

Freddie wandered to the window. "What about the Palus?" he asked. "Can't we go over there?"

Of course! Auntie Palu would take care of them! And maybe she could help make sense out of what was happening. "Let's go see," Rosie said, feeling as though a load had been lifted from her.

Freddie took hold of her hand as they walked across the grassy play area of the kindergarten that separated their house from the Palu's. How long had it been since her brother had held her hand?

Strange, thought Rosie. No one was outside on the porch at the Palu's and it seemed very quiet. Usually music played and the door opened and closed constantly as the boys, Leilani, their friends, and other relatives ran in and out.

"Are they home?" Freddie asked.

Rosie climbed the steps to the porch and knocked on the door. On any other day someone would be at the door inviting them inside before they could knock. The sound echoed emptily.

"I wanted to hear Uncle play the ukulele," Freddie said, blinking rapidly.

"Maybe the radio is back on the air and we can listen to music," Rosie said, turning and looking across to their empty house.

"I guess," Freddie mumbled.

"Let's see if the Tanakas are home," Rosie suggested, bringing up the neighbors who lived on the other side of them. They were elderly and kept more to themselves, but were always friendly.

"But they are Japs," said Freddie, holding back.

"They are our *neighbors*," Rosie said. Freddie's words made her wonder if people would say the same about them being German. No, they were as American as apple pie!

Rosie and Freddie ran across their lawn and stopped in the Tanaka's driveway. Their house was also dark and silent and their car, usually parked beside the back door, was gone.

The thought that her family might be the only one left on Oahu flitted through Rosie's mind. She quickly convinced herself how ridiculous that was, and banished the thought. However, it was very, very quiet.

As they started home, Rosie watched as one unfamiliar car and then another turned into their driveway.

Chapter 7

"Maybe that's Mama! And Papa!" Freddie yelled, letting go of Rosie's hand and running toward home.

Rosie followed. Two large black cars—not unlike the one that had carried her mama away—parked on the lawn. Not even in the driveway. The relief Rosie had let herself feel for a moment disappeared at the sight of men, more government men from the looks of them, getting out of the cars and staring at their house.

Rosie cleared her throat and croaked out, "May I help you?"

"We need to search this place," one of the men said gruffly, motioning to the others to follow him.

Rosie darted forward to stand in front of the door, ready to face another battle. She was sure Mama and Papa would never allow strangers inside. The men simply pushed open the door and stepped around her. She followed them inside, grabbing Freddie's arm and pulling him with her.

One man, who was obviously in charge of the others, gave directions, and then headed up the stairs himself. Another of the men took a position at the back door, as if blocking the way for anyone wanting to enter or exit.

An older man removed his hat and laid it on the table, revealing a bald head. He looked the least scary to Rosie. In fact, he reminded her of her Uncle Fred, who lived on a sugar plantation on the neighboring island of Kauai.

She crept over to the kitchen counter. "What are you looking for, exactly?" Rosie asked in a shaky voice.

The man glanced at her as he checked food on the shelves, shaking boxes and moving cans, searching every corner. He set aside some of the supersized cans Mama bought to feed the *kinder*.

"What do you want?" Rosie asked again, louder.

"Kid, you need to take your brother and wait in the other room. We aren't going to tell you jack shit."

Rosie jerked away from him. So, he wasn't at all like Uncle Fred, no matter what he looked like. She sat down at the kitchen table and told Freddie to do the same, taking her stand.

Soon the man in charge came downstairs carrying their camera, some of Mama's books that were written in German, and most surprising to Rosie, a gun—a big gun. Where did he find *that*?

Freddie whimpered and stood, pressing into Rosie. "Are they going to shoot us?" he whispered. "Who are they?"

Rosie shook her head, pulling her brother tighter against her side.

Another man came down carrying the radio Rosie had moved from the kitchen into the living room and a second radio that was usually in her parents' bedroom. A third man came down with their flashlights.

The bald man opened the cans he'd set aside and poured the contents into the sink, running his fingers through the food. He wiped his hands on one of Mama's towels and left the mess in the sink. "Nothing hidden in this room," he said to the man in charge.

"What are you looking for?" Rosie asked. She wondered how their belongings could help in any way with the work she had decided Mama was doing for the war. Did Mama know the men were here?

The man in charge looked at her like he was seeing her for the first time. He held out a few framed photos Rosie recognized as some of Aunt Etta's photographs that hung throughout the house. "Tell me about these," he said.

"Those—those are Tante Etta's," Rosie said,.

"Tante, huh? Is Marietta Rauschling your aunt then? And were these photographs taken in Germany?" He laid pictures on the table one at a time.

Rosie silently spelled P-H-O-T-O-G-R-A-P-H before she answered with a nod.

"And these. Did she take these photos of Pearl Harbor?" he asked, setting out another array.

Again Rosie nodded. Her aunt's photographs were beautiful. She'd had them published in newspapers and magazines.

The man gathered the framed pictures together and handed them to one of the other men, who left with them.

The bald man and the man in charge moved to the doorway leading to the classroom and talked in low voices.

"You're sure you have all the radios?" the leader called to the men who were waiting. The men nodded.

Rosie started to object—how would they know what was happening without their radios? But judging from the steely expression on the man's face, she knew her words would be useless.

With a final glance around the room at everything except Rosie and Freddie, the man pointed to the door, and everyone except the leader left carrying some piece of property belonging to the Schatzers. There was so much that Rosie couldn't keep track of all they were taking.

"Thank you for your cooperation," the man said, looking around the kitchen one last time and then tipping his hat toward Rosie.

She opened her mouth to say she would never cooperate with thieves, but instead said, "Do you know where they took our mama?" Rosie knew she both sounded and looked pathetic. Her voice shook and she had to fight to keep back the tears.

"Sorry kid, that's not my department." And he slammed the screen door behind him.

A third car waited in the road at the foot of the driveway as the two "official" cars backed out. It turned slowly toward the house.

Chapter 8

Rosie strained to make out who was inside, again hoping it was Mama or Papa. The passenger door flew open before the car came to a complete stop and for a moment she thought Mama *had* returned. But it was Tante Etta. Tante Etta had come to their rescue! Rosie had never been happier to see her.

"My darlings," Tante Etta said, going down on her knees and holding her arms open.

Without hesitation, Rosie and Freddie ran to her and buried their heads in her neck. Tante's arms felt so warm and comforting to Rosie. And she smelled so very spicy, her own special scent that she mixed herself and kept a secret. Rosie thought of it as all the wonderful scents of Hawaii.

"Are you fine? All right?" she asked, pushing them away as she stood up and looked up and down at each one of them in turn.

"They took . . . they took Mama away," Rosie said in between sobs, "And then men came, the ones leaving just now . . ."

"And they found a gun and took it!" Freddie interrupted.

"Our radios, they took—they took radios!"

Rosie tried to control her crying, but couldn't stop now that she had started. "And they took your pictures we had hanging on the wall. Why would they do that?"

At that, Tante Etta's expression changed to even more worried. "My darlings," she said with a shake of her head as she pulled Rosie to her.

Etta was her favorite tante and, Rosie was sure, Mama's favorite sister. Rosie thought Tante Etta even looked like Mama must have looked ten years ago. She was much younger and she traveled the world taking photos like the ones the men took away, dressed like a fashion model. She wasn't afraid of anything. She and her boyfriend, George, a newspaper reporter, had recently had to escape from Germany when Tante Etta accompanied him on an assignment and the war broke out in Europe. Tante Etta had made it sound like an exciting adventure, but Rosie was sure now that she had a taste of war that it probably had been more scary than exciting.

"Do you know what happened to Mama and Papa?" Rosie asked, still crying.

"I didn't know until now that anything had happened to them." Tante Etta paused. "But I have heard rumors." This time she looked behind her to where George waited in the car. She motioned for him to join them.

Freddie ran to meet George, grabbing and holding tightly to his hand.

"So tell us what has happened here." Tante Etta looked toward George again.

Rosie told them what had happened with the men driving away with Mama and that neither she nor Papa had come home or called. "But, the phone hasn't been working all the time. Maybe they tried to call." Rosie chewed on her lower lip, considering the possibility that it was the phone, not her parents, at fault. "And I thought maybe she was helping translate some German for the government. Do you think she could be doing that?"

Tante Etta took a deep breath. "We heard," she looked over her shoulder at George, who had lit a cigarette and was leaning back against the car, smoking, "but we haven't been able to confirm," she added hastily, "that the FBI is detaining some people with what they feel are German ties, as well as Japanese and Italians, that they believe or have reports of—"

Rosie interrupted. "Detain? What's that mean?" D-E-T-A-I-N. The letters appeared in her mind.

"I think—I hope it means asking questions, maybe keeping them for a while," Tante Etta said.

"But why Mama? She has no ties to Germany."

George spoke this time. "It's no secret that the FBI had

been collecting reports of suspicious activity. There has been an expectation of war for a while."

"What kind of suspicious activity? What kind of questions do they ask? Do you think they are detaining Papa, too?" Rosie said.

"Probably," George said slowly, pronouncing each syllable. "We thought," and he said it more to Tante Etta than to Rosie, "it was enemy *aliens* being rounded up."

A-L-I-E-N, Rosie spelled to herself. Her parents weren't aliens!

"'Alien' means people who aren't citizens," Tante Etta explained, "and have come from countries that are now our enemies."

"But Mama and Papa . . ."

"I know," Tante Etta said, "they are citizens." She chewed her lower lip, looking extremely upset now.

"As soon as Mama and Papa tell them they are American citizens, they'll let them go, right?" Rosie said.

Tante Etta smiled and nodded, but Rosie didn't believe that smile for a minute.

"For now, you must come with me!" Tante Etta said. "We will pack . . ."

"No, oh no! We can't leave here! What if Mama and Papa come back and we are gone? They will be so frightened. We have to stay here, Tante Etta, we must," Rosie said. She was willing to be brave enough to stay on her own if Tante Etta wouldn't agree to stay with them.

"I think, Rosie, that it would be better if you called me simply 'Etta' or 'Aunt,'" Tante suggested.

Rosie started to ask why, but the words didn't even make it to her lips before the answer came like a bolt of lightning, just like in cartoons. *Tante* was a German word—a Nazi word.

Aunt Etta pulled George aside to talk, motioning with one finger for Rosie to wait.

Rosie watched as George shrugged and returned to the car. Aunt Etta moved out of the way and waved as he backed down the driveway.

"George is going to pick up some things I might need, staying here with you, and some groceries—if he can find any," Aunt Etta said, rejoining Rosie and Freddie. "Let's go inside and we will plan a celebration for when your mama and papa arrive home."

Chapter 9

Most of that night, Rosie laid awake, thinking only the worst thoughts—that her parents were never coming back. That they might be . . . dead. Isn't that what happened to people believed to be traitors? It hadn't helped that she'd read the newspaper that George left behind when he returned with Aunt Etta's clothes. Aunt Etta had hidden the newspaper in one of the food cabinets, but Rosie had easily found it.

The news was depressing. Thousands had been killed in the bombing, and not only soldiers. The articles mentioned martial law over and over, but Rosie still wasn't sure what that was. And nowhere did it mention that people—Germans—were being taken from their homes and detained.

When she finally fell asleep, Rosie dreamed she had to evacuate—even in her dream she spelled E-V-A-C-U-A-T-E—and take only one bag. The nightmarish part was that time was ticking away and she couldn't decide what to pack. It was barely light when she startled awake, thoughts of what to pack still running through her mind.

Rosie sat up and listened. It was too quiet. She tiptoed to her parents' bedroom and saw that the bedclothes were undisturbed. Mama and Papa had not returned. Rosie crept down the stairs. Perhaps they were in the kitchen waiting to surprise her.

Aunt Etta sat at the kitchen table, alone, smoking a cigarette and painting her fingernails with red polish. She quickly stubbed out the cigarette when Rosie entered the kitchen.

Mama hated it when people smoked in the house and Aunt Etta knew it. But Rosie said nothing. Aunt Etta looked exhausted, with dark rings around her usually bright eyes. She had covered her hair with a scarf and her face was clean of any make-up. Rosie couldn't ever remember seeing her without her red lipstick. But her aunt held up the red-tipped nail polish brush. "Shall we paint your nails too?" she asked. "It always makes me feel better to have new nail polish."

Rosie nodded and laid her hand flat on the table in front of Aunt Etta. Mama said Rosie was too young to wear nail polish.

"Now let's do our toes," said Aunt Etta.

Rosie lifted her foot to Aunt Etta's knee and let her brush the polish on each toe. She admired her fingers as her aunt painted first Rosie's toes, then her own.

"We match!" said Aunt Etta, holding out her own feet next to Rosie's.

"They're so pretty and bright!" Rosie couldn't stop looking at her nails. She had always wanted to have nails like Aunt Etta's.

Aunt Etta opened her purse. "Lipstick?" She held up a shiny gold tube.

Rosie nodded. Mama didn't allow lipstick either.

Aunt Etta applied Rosie's lipstick, and then her own. "I feel better," she said, looking in her compact mirror. She turned it around and Rosie looked at herself.

She rubbed her lips together as she'd seen her mama and aunt do and then ran her tongue over her lips. They felt slick and waxy and to Rosie's surprise, the lipstick had no taste. The red color made it look like it should taste like sweet cherries.

"Oooh! You look like you should be in high school at least," Aunt Etta said, making Rosie giggle.

"It takes more than nail polish and lipstick to do that," said Rosie, although the make-up did make her feel more grown-up. And the war was making her feel like she had to *be* more grown-up.

"Seventh grade, then," said her aunt. "Do you want some breakfast?"

"No thank you." Rosie sat across from her aunt. "Any word?"

"George asked at the newspaper and spoke to some of his contacts. Because of the island being under martial law, there have been arrests, mostly Japanese community leaders, but some folks of German or Italian backgrounds that the government thinks might be a threat as well. Japan, Germany, and Italy are all in this war." Aunt Etta leaned across the table and spoke very seriously to Rosie, making her feeling of being grown-up more real.

Rosie knew all too well the world was at war. But there was much she didn't understand. "I keep reading Hawaii is under martial law. But I don't know what that means," she said.

"Basically, it means that the military is in charge."

"So, it's the military who took Mama and Papa?" Rosie was still confused because the men wore suits, not uniforms. "Did they take them because of their German name? Do they, whoever they are, truly think that Mama and Papa are . . ." Rosie hesitated, "Nazis?"

"I don't know what *they* are thinking, sweetheart. I find it as ridiculous as you do, but evidently they believe they have some reason . . ."

"No! There is no reason," Rosie said. Tears threatened again. "George needs to do something."

"He is trying to find out what he can, like where your parents are being held, first of all," said Aunt Etta.

"Tell him thank you, please," Rosie said. "What about Tante—I mean, *Aunt* Yvonne?"

"Uncle Charles isn't German and his family is very prominent on Oahu. The Bell family has lived here for generations. She is no doubt safe. I tried to call her, too, but I can't get through."

"But your family, the Rauschlings, have been here forever, too! You know that. And I thought that in America, people couldn't be arrested for no reason, and that the government couldn't just walk into your house and take whatever they wanted," said Rosie, feeling angry. "We studied the Constitution in school."

"It's different days now. We are at war, and like I said, the Army is making all the rules," Aunt Etta explained. "That can happen in times of war."

Rosie tried to make sense of what she was hearing her aunt say, but all she ended with was that war wasn't good for her family.

Aunt Etta's next words were drowned out by the sound of a car pulling up to the house. "George," Aunt Etta said, blushing slightly and smiling broadly. She hurried to the screen door, but instead of opening it, she froze, staring at the driveway.

"Is it Mama and Papa?" Rosie asked, running to her aunt's side. She felt cold all over when she recognized the car and the man standing beside it. It was the government man who had taken Mama away.

Rosie pushed at Aunt Etta. "Quick!" she said, "Run! Get away. Hide! Do something!" Rosie tried to close the door to lock it.

But Aunt Etta could not be moved. She had turned an ugly shade of pale.

Rosie turned back around and the man was on the other side of the screen door.

"Miss Rauschling?" he asked, "Marietta Rauschling?"

Aunt Etta nodded, but said nothing.

"No!" Rosie shouted at the man, "That's not her name. This is our . . . nurse, staying with us because you took our mama away."

Aunt Etta placed her hand on Rosie's head. "Shh! Darling, don't tell lies."

Lies! Somebody had told lies already. Why else would her family be taken away?

Freddie had crept down the stairs to the door and stood to the side.

"Aunt Etta, no! You can't go, too." Rosie turned to the man in the doorway, "Where are you taking my aunt? What are you going to do with her? Where is my Mama? Is she alive? Just tell me if my mama is alive," she begged.

"We have a few questions for you, Miss Rauschling, that's all," the man said as he pulled the screen door open and took hold of Aunt Etta's arm.

"Rosie, you must call Aunt Yvonne when you can get through. And George. Or have Yvonne call George. And you must take care of Freddie and yourself. I'm sure that I will return soon." She pulled Rosie to her and kissed the top of her head, then grabbed Freddie and gave him a tight hug. She looked hard at the man waiting to take her away. "After all," she said, squaring her shoulders, "I haven't done anything wrong."

"No!" Rosie shouted, following as Aunt Etta was led to

the car. She grabbed her aunt around the waist and held on. "Don't go, please don't leave us here. Please. I'm scared."

The man gently peeled Rosie off her aunt.

Rosie collapsed on the ground. "Don't go!" she yelled after the car. "Please don't go!" she called, sobbing. Rosie remained on the ground even after the car disappeared, crying as she pulled up handfuls of grass. They were alone again.

Chapter 10

"Rosie?" She felt Freddie's hand on her shoulder.

Rosie couldn't move; her sadness was too heavy. It was hard to be brave when she felt all alone.

"The phone is working. I checked. Let's go call Tante—I mean, Aunt Yvonne," he said. His face was tear-streaked and his nose ran. He rubbed the back of his hand across his face, smearing wetness all over.

Aunt Yvonne. Their older, proper aunt. She lived in a big house in Honolulu and entertained her bridge club with stale cake and tea. Mama had gone once or twice when they needed another player, but she never had anything good to say about the parties. Rosie wanted Aunt Etta if she couldn't have Mama. She couldn't remember Aunt Yvonne ever giving them a hug or doing anything but telling them NOT to do something.

"Rosie?" Freddie said again. "Aunt Etta made us some breakfast. I ate mine but yours is still on the table."

"I'll come inside in a minute," Rosie said, wiping her face. She needed some time to gather herself before she called Aunt Yvonne.

Freddie nodded and walked to the porch, where he sat with his head resting on his knees.

Rosie knew that Aunt Yvonne would not come to their house to stay with them. They would have to go into town and stay at her most proper home. She half-hoped the phone wouldn't work as she slowly walked inside. Freddie looked so sad, she paused and gave him a quick hug. He hugged her back, tightly, a big change from the way he had been before it was just the two of them. Before the bombing that started the war. She guessed that was the way time would be measured for her going forward: before the war and after the war. When she had a family, and when she was on her own.

The phone buzzed in her ear as she lifted it, and the operator came on asking for the number. Rosie recited Aunt Yvonne's number and listened to the phone ring.

"Hello?" her aunt answered.

"It's me, Rosie."

"Hello, dear. How are you and Greta? Freddie? Henry?"

Rosie swallowed a sob at the mention of her mother and father. "Mama and Papa were taken away. At least we think Papa was. He went to work and he hasn't come back. Men came and took Mama, and this morning they took Aunt Etta."

Silence met Rosie's report of what had been happening at their house.

"All of them," Aunt Yvonne finally said, "taken?"

Rosie nodded, and then realized her aunt couldn't possibly see her. "Yes," she said, then added, "ma'am."

"Who is taking care of you and Freddie? One of the teachers from the kindergarten?"

"No, no one," Rosie said. "Aunt Etta said to call you. And she wants you to call George at the newspaper to tell him what happened, too."

"She is still dating that Jewish man?" Aunt Yvonne said. "Heavens. What to do, what to do," she mumbled. "It's all happening again."

Rosie had no idea what her aunt was talking about. What was happening again? She took a deep breath. "Aunt Yvonne, would you come out here and stay with us until Mama and Papa come back?"

"Oh, I couldn't possibly. I have far too many responsibilities here, my dear. But, I suppose, yes, I guess I must. You and Freddie must stay here. You certainly cannot stay alone in the valley. Pack a few things, for surely it won't be long once they find out there is no reason to detain your father and mother. Rainer will drive out and pick you up. You hear me, Roselie? Be ready and he will come in the car to bring you here."

"Yes, ma'am," Rosie replied, not at all happy with her aunt's solution to their problem.

"I will see you soon, then. I must prepare." The phone clicked and her aunt was gone.

Rosie sat at the table and twirled the plate of cinnamon toast her Aunt Etta had made for her breakfast. She took a bite and although she swallowed hard, it stuck in her throat. "Freddie, are you still hungry?" she called out the door.

"For what?" he asked, coming inside.

"I'm not really hungry this morning." She held out her cinnamon toast.

"Did you talk to Aunt Yvonne?" Freddie asked, his mouth stuffed with toast.

"She's sending Rainer to pick us up. So, pack whatever you think you will need."

Freddie made a face, probably because of their cousin Rainer. He had never been very nice to them, and there was no reason to believe he would start now.

Rosie cleaned Kitty's food and water bowls and packed them with her cat food. Kitty had been curled on her bed the last time she saw her. She'd bring the cat downstairs but make her stay inside so she would be easy to find when Rainer arrived.

Upstairs, Rosie looked for a suitcase but decided they didn't need anything that big. "Use your schoolbag to pack your stuff," she called downstairs to Freddie. "And you'd better come on up and pick out what you want to take. You know Rainer will be mad if we aren't ready. He may make us go with him whether we're ready or not."

At that, Freddie clattered up the steps.

Rosie picked out three books from her Nancy Drew series, hoping she wouldn't be away from home any longer than it would take her to read them. She sat on the bed and stared at the mysteries. Here she was right in the middle of the biggest mystery of her life—where were her parents? Would Nancy wait to see what happened if Carson Drew was dragged off by a man in a black suit? Would Nancy sit around and wonder why her mama and papa had disappeared or would she investigate? Maybe she should take a clue from Nancy instead of waiting to see what everyone else might do. It would be easier once she made it to Aunt Yvonne's house in the middle of town. As much as she loved living at the edge of town, it wasn't always the most convenient place.

Rosie tucked the books in her bag along with clean underwear, a clean dress, her hairbrush, ribbons, toothbrush, and shoes. She figured Aunt Yvonne would make her wear shoes. Giving one more look around her bedroom, she carried her bag to the kitchen to wait.

And wait. And wait.

"Can't I please go outside?" Freddie begged over and over. Tired of hearing him, Rosie finally said yes but cautioned him about wandering away.

She carried their schoolbags and Kitty's food outside to the porch. Rosie stared at the road and willed her cousin to appear, but only one bicycler rode by the house.

Finally, a car horn honked from the driveway.

Rosie saw her cousin Rainer with a girl sitting beside him—really close beside him. They were kissing. Yuck.

Tucking Kitty under her arm, she pulled the door shut behind her and locked it, then placed the key on the ledge under the porch.

Freddie had already picked up his bag, climbed into the car, and was hanging over the front seat, talking to Rainer and the girl.

Rosie hoisted her bag over her shoulder and grabbed the bag with Kitty's food and bowls.

"Hey!" Rainer leaned out the car window. "You aren't taking that cat with you."

"I can't leave her here alone!" Rosie said, tears threatening once again.

"Mom would have a fit if you brought that thing into her house," Rainer said. He shook his head. "No, you can't bring it." He opened the car door, took Kitty from Rosie and threw her to the ground.

"Stop! You'll hurt her." Rosie leaned down and talked softly to her cat. "It won't be long, Kitty, and I will leave plenty of food and some water."

Rosie dug the key out of the hiding place and went back inside. She found two of Mama's biggest bowls in the cabinet and filled them with food and water. She carried the water carefully and placed it under the porch where she knew Kitty liked to rest. After she placed the food bowl near the water, she gave Kitty a last hug and relocked the door.

"C'mon, c'mon, c'mon," Rainer yelled.

Rosie settled in the back seat beside Freddie and wished she had hidden Kitty in her schoolbag. She would a thousand times rather have her cat with her than clean clothes. But it was too late now.

"Maybe we could stop by the Palus and ask them to check on Kitty," Rosie suggested.

Rainer ignored her. "This is Lily," he said, his arm around the girl with long dark hair and dark skin. "She's my secret, meaning do not mention you saw me with a girl in the car to Mom. Because if you do, I will make sure you end up in an orphanage where you belong. Think about that while we drive Lily home."

O-R-P-H-A-N-A-G-E. Rainer said mean things so often, Rosie knew not to pay attention to them.

Rosie steeled herself for whatever was to come. She was dry-eyed as she watched Kitty sitting on the back porch, cleaning her face, until she became the tiniest of tiny orange dots. No Mama, no Papa, no Kitty, and no more tears.

Chapter 11

"There are some rules that the two of you will need to follow," Aunt Yvonne announced before Rosie and Freddie had stepped completely inside the house.

Rosie stared at the soft blue rug with large flowers woven into it that covered the hall floor. She felt Freddie slip his hand into hers.

"First, when I tell you to be ready at a certain time, you need to be ready. I had several things on the schedule for Rainer to do today but since he had to wait for you to be ready to come with him, those things will have to be added to tomorrow's schedule. This is a very busy household."

Rosie glared at Rainer, leaning against the wall smirking at the two of them. That they weren't ready to leave was his excuse for being gone so long, when the truth was he had been with his secret girlfriend.

"Second, and this is very important, you are not to mention to anyone where your parents are. It's a scandal to have
my sisters incarcerated. We will say you are . . ." Aunt Yvonne
paused and looked away, "refugees that we have taken in."

Rosie was speechless. She hadn't expected alohas or mountains of leis from Aunt Yvonne, but she also didn't expect her
own aunt to deny that she was family.

Aunt Yvonne continued, "We need to be cautious. We
don't know if someone is watching us."

Watching them? Rosie thought her aunt was letting her
imagination—I-M-A-G-I-N-A-T-I-O-N—get the best of her.

"And finally, I know you run amuck on that property in
the middle of nowhere, but here you must stay close by. Where
are your shoes?"

Rosie curled her toes and pressed her feet together. "In my
bag," she admitted.

Aunt Yvonne shook her head. "We wear shoes on our feet
in Honolulu, not nail polish. There is a bottle of remover in
my bathroom. Please take it off. Now."

Rosie covered one of her bare feet with the other. If Aunt
Yvonne said they would wear shoes, Rosie figured they would
wear shoes.

"Uncle Charles is trying to find out what has happened
to your parents. Lord knows he has enough else to do! We
aren't at all sure we can do anything, but he will try," Aunt
Yvonne said more gently. "Now, you will have to share a room,
so go upstairs with Rainer and clean up before supper. That

includes removing that hideous nail polish." She directed her last remark at Rosie before disappearing into the shadows of the room to the left of the hallway.

"Aunt Yvonne!" Rosie called after her.

"What is it?" her aunt replied but did not return.

Speaking into the shadows, Rosie said, "Rainer said I couldn't bring my cat with me. Can't I please have Kitty here? She's never had to be on her own before."

"Rosie, we have no place for a cat here. They shed all over and if we tried to leave her outside, she would run away. If your parents aren't back in a few days, I will make sure someone checks on the cat."

"That would be me," Rainer said under his breath, frowning at Rosie.

"Aunt Yvonne, please . . ."

"No. I can't take on one more responsibility. No cats," Aunt Yvonne said shrilly and Rosie heard her footsteps fade as she walked deeper into the house.

Rosie felt tears burn, but willed herself not to cry. It did no good and she wouldn't let her aunt see her weakness.

"C'mon," Rainer took the stairs two at a time while Rosie and Freddie followed slowly, Freddie still holding tightly to Rosie's hand.

Rainer threw open a door at the end of the hall. "This is it. Believe me, you'd better follow all the rules Mom set out if you don't want to go to the you-know-where."

"I don't want to go to an orphanist," Freddie whispered.

"Aunt Yvonne won't make us go anyplace. And Rainer is just trying to scare us." Rosie stared hard at her cousin. "We'll stay right here until Mama and Papa come for us."

"This is your bathroom and this is mine." Rainer pointed at doors on opposite sides of the hallway.

Rosie leaned around Rainer to peek inside his room. She couldn't believe what was hanging on his wall. "Do you go to Punahou?" She stepped across the threshold to look more closely at the pennant hanging over his desk.

Rainer blocked Rosie from coming all the way into his room. "Yeah, I do. So what?"

Rosie swallowed hard. "I'm applying to go there next year," she said. Her enthusiasm for the school dampened slightly, knowing her cousin attended. Were all the students like him? She wouldn't have a chance to find out if Mama and Papa didn't return to finish the application. Why did the war complicate life so?

"Good luck," Rainer said, then he slammed his door.

Rosie glared at Rainer's door as she pushed Freddie into the room they would share. White walls, a white chenille bedspread with a big pineapple design in the middle, a white rug beside the bed covering the shiny wood floor, and a low bureau against the wall. The room was very small and very dark. Rosie could barely scoot between the bureau and the bed to get to the window to open the shade. When light streamed in, she realized Aunt Yvonne had already hung extra dark shades required for blackouts. At least that meant she could have a light and read at night.

The room overlooked the roof of the back porch and the patch of green grass that grew past the porch, surrounded by banks of brightly colored flowers. Mama would know the names of every one. Love of gardening was the one thing she and Aunt Yvonne shared.

Freddie sat on the opposite edge of the bed, holding his schoolbag. "I didn't bring any shoes," he said, tears shining in his eyes.

"Aunt Yvonne will have to give in on her rule or take you to buy a pair," Rosie said with a shrug.

"I'm afraid to tell her," Freddie admitted.

"Don't be. It's a silly rule. We never wear shoes at home." Rosie didn't feel as sure of her aunt's acceptance of their bare feet as her words sounded. "I won't wear shoes either, so she'll have to be mad at both of us. Okay?" It was a battle, a small battle, she would fight for her brother. She also wasn't ready to give up her fight for Kitty.

Freddie answered slowly, "Okay. I guess. At least then she'll send both of us to the orphanist."

"Orphanage," Rosie corrected him. "But don't listen to Rainer. He's a bully."

Freddie shrugged.

"It will be all right," Rosie said, reaching across the bed to touch her brother's shoulder. And again her words sounded much more confident than Rosie felt.

Chapter 12

The days dragged by until a week had passed since they had arrived at their aunt's house. Aunt Yvonne had to give in on her must-wear-shoes rule since Freddie had none, but she did not budge on letting them leave the house beyond the back-yard—at least when she was home. The yard and house were plenty big enough for Freddie to play his never-ending game of war, but Rosie soon tired of the limits and of war, play or otherwise.

She hoped that one of Freddie's Christmas presents would be the little Army men he talked about all the time. She felt sad every time she saw him gather sticks and rocks to use as soldiers. And she hoped one of her gifts would be a new journal. Rosie couldn't believe she'd forgotten to pack hers. Actually, Rosie hoped she, or at least Freddie, would have *any* kind of gift.

And, she missed her friends, especially Leilani. Not being able to see and talk to her best friend made everything harder. Aunt Yvonne had put the telephone off-limits to keep the line open for "important" calls, so she couldn't call her. The only good thing about the rule was that it applied to Rainer, too.

And what if Leilani was still mad at her? They hadn't had a chance to work things out before she had to leave. Rosie hated the feeling that there was something unfinished between them.

Together she and Leilani could surely figure out what to do to bring Mama and Papa home. Or at least figure out why they'd been taken. No one yet, including Rosie herself, had been able to come up with that answer.

She *could* write to her friend.

Rosie tiptoed into her aunt's bedroom and found stationery—S-T-A-T-I-O-N-E-R-Y—and an envelope in the desk. She sat down, checking first to make sure no one else was upstairs, and quickly wrote Leilani a note.

Dear Leilani,

We are staying with our Aunt Yvonne. Mama, Papa, and Aunt Etta were taken away for questions and I don't know where they are now! I wish you were here to help me figure out all the questions I have—where? Why? When will they return? We could be like Nancy Drew! I hope we will be home soon, but maybe Auntie Palu could bring you here to see us.

I miss you so much.
Aloha, Rosie

Rosie folded the letter and tucked it in the envelope, deciding not to say anything about Leilani being mad at her. She was probably over it by now. At least Rosie hoped so. She addressed the envelope, then searched for a postage stamp. Nothing. She would have to ask Aunt Yvonne.

Later that afternoon when her aunt appeared, Rosie handed her the letter and asked if she would please mail it. Aunt Yvonne put it into her purse with a sigh.

"Rosie! Freddie!" Aunt Yvonne called for them later the same day.

Rosie came downstairs, wondering what her aunt needed now. Freddie was already waiting in the hallway.

"We have to register the two of you for identification cards. And pick up your gas masks. Once we have them, you must carry them with you at all times. Come. Now." Aunt Yvonne held the door open as they filed out of the house and climbed into the car.

When Aunt Yvonne parked the car in front of the local school, she turned around. "Remember," she said, "you are refugees we have taken in due to the war."

The thought that her own family didn't want to claim her as kin made Rosie sad. But she had come to expect little out of Aunt Yvonne.

The woman who registered them, Mrs. Smith, was a friend of her aunt's who taught at the school.

Mrs. Smith thought it lovely of Aunt Yvonne to take in refugees! Rosie wanted to throw up.

"When do you think school will resume?" Aunt Yvonne asked the teacher as she filled out the cards for her "refugees." Rosie thought she heard what sounded like desperation in her aunt's voice.

"They've assigned all teachers and school personnel to work issuing identification cards," Mrs. Smith said, "and that is a big job. I would expect sometime after the holidays." Mrs. Smith did not look happy that school would start up again that soon.

"Not till next year?" Aunt Yvonne sounded equally unhappy at the date.

Rosie realized, looking around the gym, if they stayed with Aunt Yvonne, she and Freddie would attend this new school, where she knew no one.

"Can you mail my letter now?" Rosie asked as they returned to the car.

"I will send it with Uncle Charles when he goes to work tomorrow. This day has worn me out," Aunt Yvonne said.

Rosie and Freddie exchanged looks. Rosie hadn't seen her aunt do anything all day besides sit and read magazines.

The day after they received their gas masks and identification cards, Rosie came downstairs to find only the hired girl, Kealani, in the kitchen. It was so strange to have someone cleaning up after them and always hovering about. Rosie was used to making her own bed and helping Mama with other chores. Aunt Yvonne made sure to mention they would have to pay Kealani more for all the extra work Rosie and Freddie made. Rosie realized, listening to Aunt Yvonne, that Rainer came by his ability to make people feel bad with words naturally.

Kealani was bent over a square of cloth stretched tightly in a wooden hoop. She jumped up and dropped the square behind her onto the chair where she had been sitting.

"Is that a quilt?" Rosie asked, reaching around the young girl and picking up her work.

"I have finished the cleaning and am waiting for the washing to end," Kealani said.

"I don't care if you're quilting. This is pretty." Rosie held up the square with a pink flower design in the middle. "My mama was working on a Hawaiian quilt."

"Do you quilt, too?" Kealani looked interested in her for the first time since they'd arrived, Rosie thought.

"Oh, no." Rosie shook her head.

"But you could. You should!"

Rosie turned Kealani's quilt square around looking at it from every side. "It's too hard."

"They aren't all this complicated." This quilt square was sprays of flowers, very intricate, and Kealani's stitches were tiny, tiny the way Auntie Palu always stressed they should be. "I could teach you, if you want. And, it would give you something to do besides sit around and worry about your parents."

"How do you know that's all I do?" Rosie asked. She read, she pulled weeds, and when she could find paper, she wrote— journal entries and lists of spelling words from a dictionary she'd found on a shelf in the living room.

"I notice more that goes on in this house than you might imagine," said Kealani. "And right now, I feel the loneliness and unhappiness the war brings. I will bring you fabric and teach you." She took back her quilt square and sat down, stitching once again. "Your breakfast is on the counter," she added.

"Where's Aunt Yvonne?" Rosie asked as she shoved in bites of the pineapple, fish, and fried rice dish that Kealani had prepared. It was so much better than the cooked rice cereal that Aunt Yvonne usually served. "Aunt Yvonne?" she asked again.

"All day gone," the girl answered. She smiled broadly.

Rosie glanced out the window and it was another blue sky Hawaii day, perfect for what she had in mind. She quickly ate the remainder of her breakfast and rushed upstairs.

She brushed her hair and put on her shoes. Peeking around the corner of the doorway, Rosie made sure Rainer was also gone. She tiptoed into his room and headed straight for the brightly painted mug on his bureau. She'd seen him drop change into the mug each evening when he came home. She reached inside and felt around the bottom, pulling out several coins. She would need money for the streetcar.

"Whatcha doing?"

Rosie whirled around, startled. It was Freddie.

"Shh, I'm going to try to find out something about where Mama and Papa are," she whispered, checking over her brother's shoulder into the hallway.

"I want to help," said Freddie.

Rosie shook her head and started to push past her brother.

"Look, Rosie, Rainer has a ukulele. I haven't played one in so long." Freddie picked up the small stringed instrument off the bureau top.

"You? Play?" Rosie laughed.

"I can," said Freddie.

"Still you should ask before you take that," Rosie warned.

"Did you ask if you could take that money?" He ran his fingers across the strings and released music.

"It's different," Rosie tried to explain.

Freddie carried the ukulele into their bedroom and sat on the bed, strumming it to make different sounds.

"Make sure you put it back before Rainer or Aunt Yvonne see it," said Rosie. "And I will be back before then, too." She ran lightly down the stairs and slipped out the front door.

Chapter 13

Even though Christmas was coming, there were no trees in the windows of the homes she passed. The boat from the mainland carrying Christmas trees had never arrived in Hawaii so people were either doing without or hanging decorations from coconut or palm fronds. She missed the traditional holiday cheer but knew most people, including herself, weren't feeling very cheery.

Rosie had seen the streetcar pass at the end of Aunt Yvonne's street many times as she sat and watched out the window, waiting and hoping for her parents to come back. She had even ridden the streetcar to visit her aunt with her mama when the two of them were on better terms. She ran when she heard the car coming and climbed on board, dropping change into the container beside the driver.

Sitting stiffly and staring straight ahead, Rosie had the

strange feeling that her aunt or Rainer might pass the streetcar and see her riding away. She decided not to care.

The streetcar reached King Street, the heart of shopping in Honolulu, and Rosie hopped off the bus. She took a few minutes to look around. In earlier Decembers, her family had made a special trip to see the holiday decorations, but this year it would be a wasted trip. A few shops had bells or glass Christmas balls hanging, but more shocking to see was the tape across every window. To keep them from breaking in case more bombs were dropped? Some inventive storekeepers had made the tape into decorations—a V for victory, or bells, or wreaths. There were also sandbags piled against buildings, narrowing the sidewalks. The changes combined to make Rosie feel like she was in a place she'd never been.

Rosie slowly turned down the side street where her father's radio shop was located, nervous about what she might find. Pausing, she pictured Papa behind the counter, dusting off the shiny cases and running his hand over their smooth wood. Despite all the people walking past, Rosie was filled to bursting with the loneliness of missing Mama and Papa. Even the cutout of a radio that hung over the sidewalk marking the shop's door appeared lonely.

Rosie turned the doorknob. The door was locked. She stepped closer to the window and pressed her face against the glass. The shelves were empty.

No Papa. No radios. And those men had taken all the radios from their home as well. Rosie realized with a start that the radios must be at least part of the reason her parents had been taken away.

Had the FBI suspected that Papa was using his radios against his country?

Rosie stepped away from the radio shop, and as she looked up and down the street wondering where to go next, a sudden whine filled the air—the wavering tones of an air raid siren. Rosie panicked. What to do? Where to hide?

Chapter 14

At Aunt Yvonne's when the sirens blared, she had them huddle in the downstairs hallway, complaining until the all clear sounded and they could return to bed or to whatever they'd been doing. So far, the sirens had been drills only.

Here, people rushed by, all headed in one direction toward the far end of the street and what she only could imagine was a shelter.

Was this a drill or was it again the "real McCoy"? As Rosie tried to decide where to go, a boy who looked to be around her age grabbed her hand and pulled her into the flow of people running.

"Don't just stand there," he said.

"I don't know where . . ." Rosie tried to pull her hand out of his grip.

"There's a shelter at the end of the street," he said as they joined the crush of people, shoppers and shopkeepers, flowing down a set of cement steps.

Once at the bottom, the boy continued to move Rosie along through the press of people filling the tunnel until he found a bare space and pressed himself against the wall. Rosie remained where they'd stopped until he pushed her back beside him. "It's a drill," he said into her ear. "But if one of the wardens finds you standing in the open, you could be in big trouble."

"You're sure it's a drill?" Rosie said, her throat dry. Under the ground as they were, the mixed scents of the crowd's perfumes and body odors on top of the mustiness made her feel slightly sick.

The boy nodded. "Did you see any airplanes?"

Rosie tried to remember and couldn't recall seeing—or hearing—a thing beyond the siren.

"I'm Kam," he said. "Are you new around here?"

"The radio shop—" she began, then cut off her words. No need to tell anyone that the shop belonged to her dad, although she immediately felt guilty for keeping it a secret, as if she was ashamed. "I was shopping," Rosie mumbled.

"What's your name?" Kam asked.

"Rosie," she said quietly.

"I love this long vacation from school. Don't you? I mean, except for the war and everything."

Rosie nodded, although being at Aunt Yvonne's didn't feel much like a vacation.

"My auntie that I live with used to make leis for the tourists. Now she weaves nets to camouflage the buildings. I run errands for her and the rest of the aunties. It's something to do and they pay me," he said with a grin. "Do your folks work around here?"

Rosie shook her head, again ashamed she didn't have the nerve to be honest.

Kam slid down the wall and sat on the floor. Rosie joined him, finding the cement floor damp against her legs and bottom.

"I guess there aren't a lot of tourists wanting leis these days," Rosie said to keep the conversation going and to keep her mind off what could be happening above ground, if it wasn't a drill.

"There are still some tourists here, left behind since the boats are afraid to make the trip back to the mainland. And there are the soldiers, more every day. I mean, I'm with my auntie because my dad is stranded on the mainland and hasn't been able to make it back to the islands. He travels a lot."

"That must be awful! For the people stranded here and for your dad."

"But they are a part of history," said Kam, tapping his foot. "All of us here are."

Rosie shrugged.

"Just like my auntie tells me over and over about the day Liliuokalani stepped down from ruling the islands and turned them over to the United States, we'll be telling our kids and grandkids about December 7, a date which will live in infamy."

Rosie had never thought that far into the future when she considered the bombing. All she knew was that it led to her parents being taken away from her.

The all clear sounded and Kam stood up, brushing the back of his shorts. Rosie stood and smoothed her skirt.

"This shelter is much better than having to dive into one of the ditches that they've dug for people to jump into when there is an air raid," Kam said. "Do you have a shelter where you live?"

Rosie shook her head. Aunt Yvonne said she'd had to ruin the inside of her house with blackout curtains, and she didn't intend to ruin the outside by digging up her flowers for ditches that wouldn't keep them safe from anything anyway. Rosie agreed with her about the ditches.

"I didn't say—I-I never said thank you," Rosie stammered. "For showing me the way down here." *And keeping my mind off the possibility of bombs falling all around* remained unsaid.

"Hey, I wouldn't want to see you carted off to the pokey." Kam punched her lightly on the arm. "C'mon, I'll show you the way back. Were you going to buy a radio or something from that old German? I hope you weren't expecting to pick up one you left for repair!"

Rosie didn't like how he spoke of her father, dismissing him as an "old German." Kam didn't even know him. "That 'old German' is my father and that is his shop," she finally summoned the courage to admit. "He's the radio king of Hawaii."

"Oops. Sorry, I didn't know I was in the presence of royalty." Kam bowed. "And I guess he wasn't that old." He grinned at her.

It was hard for Rosie not to smile back, so she gave in.

They reached the street and the sun almost blinded Rosie. She blinked her eyes, trying to adjust to the brightness.

"My auntie saw the government men take him away. What did he do?" Kam asked, holding Rosie's arm as she tried to walk away.

This was why she didn't want Kam to know she was connected to the shop. How to answer? So many thoughts were mixing around in her head. Finally, she decided to be honest.

"Nothing! He did nothing! At first I thought maybe they took him to help translate something in German, but now, after seeing his shop empty, I wonder if the radios have something to do with his . . ." she faltered, "detainment."

Kam nodded, looking thoughtful. "They took a bunch of Japs away too," he offered. "Maybe they thought your dad was broadcasting information to Germany, Hitler even, on one of the radios."

Rosie jerked her arm away and faced Kam, her hands on her hips. Why had she opened herself to this boy she'd barely met? At least now she knew how people would react to news of her father and mother being taken away. Exactly the way she'd feared.

"Radios are his business. They're what he knows. I told

you, he's the radio king of Hawaii. And he would never be disloyal to America."

"Hey, I believe you," said Kam.

Did he? Rosie still wasn't sure whether or not to trust the boy. But who else did she have to confide her suspicions to—S-U-S-P-I-C-I-O-N-S? Aunt Yvonne refused to discuss Mama and Papa. And Rainer, she knew better than to talk to him about anything.

"But if it was the radios, why did they take my mama?" Rosie felt her throat tighten. "She barely knows how to turn on a radio."

"You know, we are all supposed to be on the lookout for spies. Maybe someone saw your father do something they didn't understand and made a report to the FBI," Kam said. "The FBI came and talked to the aunties one day. They see and hear all kinds of stuff. The men said they could make a report and not have to give their name if they didn't want to. I imagine there are lots of reports being made these days, too, too many to look into too much," said Kam.

Aunt Etta had said the FBI was collecting reports of anything suspicious, but Rosie hadn't realized until now that that meant *citizens* being asked to report anything suspicious. Had someone made a report to the FBI about Papa and his radios? If so, that person had certainly lied about Papa's work and loyalty. Rosie took a deep breath and looked carefully at everyone passing by. The fact that any unknown person could report that they suspected her Papa and Mama of doing something disloyal and that is likely what led to them being taken away by the government made her doubt everything she had learned in school about D-E-M-O-C-R-A-C-Y.

"So, did your auntie think she saw something at my father's shop?" Rosie asked.

"They haven't ever made a report on anything."

"Who would? Who does?" Rosie said.

"Lots of people hate Germans these days. And they hate Japs even more," Kam said.

"Being German, just *being* German can't be enough," said Rosie. "And besides, Mama and Papa are American!" How many times would she have to say that before anyone believed her?

Church bells rang out the hour and, startled, Rosie realized it was growing late. This trip had at least given her something to think about and to investigate—I-N-V-E-S-T-I-G-A-T-E. She needed to find out *who* would report on her mama and papa. And with all her heart and mind, Rosie knew whatever her parents had been accused of doing, they hadn't done it.

Rosie was hesitant to go. It felt good to talk to someone her own age. She turned toward the streetcar stop and saw a bus approaching.

"If you're ever back around here, just ask Auntie to give me a yell. She'll be weaving nets and I'll, well, I'll be around." Again, Kam grinned.

Rosie waved as she ran to catch the streetcar. She sat back, breathless, and tried to sort her thoughts. By the time she reached Aunt Yvonne's, she had convinced herself the radios were definitely connected to her papa's detainment. Now all she had to do was figure out what to do next.

She felt like Nancy Drew at the beginning of a case. It was a mystery for sure: the who, what, and why of her parents' detainment. Rosie didn't, however, believe it would be as easy for her as it was for Nancy to find out the answers.

Rosie missed her journal. The first thing she would do when she reached Aunt Yvonne's was find some more paper. Writing her thoughts always made them clearer.

At the front door, she paused as ukulele music drifted down the steps. That couldn't be Freddie!

Rosie hurried upstairs and stood outside their bedroom door, listening. The melody was simple, but sounded pure Hawaiian, reminding her of soft breezes blowing through the trees and waves gently greeting them on a visit to the beach.

Freddie looked up from the instrument when Rosie entered the bedroom. And it *was* only Freddie. "What? Where did you . . . ?"

"Uncle Palu taught me. And I really miss the ukulele. And him." Freddie laid the instrument on the bed beside him.

"I didn't know you played."

Freddie shrugged and slid off the bed, picking up the ukulele on the way. "I'll put it back now."

"That was good, Freddie," Rosie said.

Freddie grinned. "I know."

Chapter 15

Rosie knew it was wrong, but she found a blank spiral note-book in a drawer near the telephone and took it. She wrote:

Dear Nancy Drew,

I need your help. My parents were taken away and I want to know why. Here is a list of what I know:

All of Papa's radios, at home and at the shop, were taken

Papa speaks with a German accent still

We have a German name

The FBI is collecting reports about suspicious activities that might hurt us in the war

And here is a list of my questions:

Who made the report?

Why did someone make a report?

*And why Mama and Tante—*she marked out *Tante—Aunt Etta?*

Where? Where are they? If I could only see them to make sure they are all right.

If Carson Drew were missing, what would you do first to find him? Don't say "ask your friends and relatives" because they have no more idea where my parents are than I do! I went to the last place I knew Papa had gone and it is completely empty. If you're up for a trip to Honolulu, I sure could use your help.

Aloha, Rosie

Now all she had to do was wait for Nancy to show up to help. Or Leilani. Surely she had received the letter by now! The two of them had always wanted to find a good mystery to solve and here was one. Rosie looked at her list. It might be too much for her.

Rosie put down her pencil. She was hungry. Hopefully, Kealani had fixed their lunch. Aunt Yvonne had little imagination when it came to cooking. She missed Mama's delicious German meals, as well as the tasty Hawaiian dishes Auntie Palu had taught her mother to cook.

Rosie slowly walked down the stairs, humming a song Mama often played for the *kinder* in her school. She also missed those little rascals.

"Rosie, is that you dear?" Aunt Yvonne called from the living room.

Rosie leaned against the wall, "It's me, Aunt," she answered.

"Come here for a moment. There's someone you should meet."

As Rosie entered the living room a woman dressed in a faded dress and woven sandals sat up straighter in her corner of the sofa. Her aunt was going to actually let her talk to someone?

"This *Frau*—I mean, Mrs. Launius. She has something for you. Something you will be very happy to receive," Aunt Yvonne said in a soft voice, much softer than her normal tone.

"Mrs. Launius, it is very nice to meet you," Rosie said, standing tall in front of the woman.

"You are as lovely as your mother described," Mrs. Launius said in a heavily German accented voice.

"You . . . you've talked to my mother?"

Mrs. Launius nodded. "And she sent this. And please to know, this is the second try to send a note to her *kinder*. The first time was not secret."

Rosie grabbed the scrap of paper Mrs. Launius held out. It was folded into a tiny package and smelled of cigarettes. One side of the paper looked to be a printed laundry list. On the other side, she recognized her mother's writing, very cramped.

Rosie read eagerly, her heart beating quickly.

My darlings, Papa, Etta, and I are fine. We are being held at Ft. Armstrong, in case no one has told you, as enemy aliens. Of course, we are neither alien nor enemy. George and Uncle

Charles are working hard to obtain our release along with Etta's. We will be so sad not to spend the holidays with you but know that Aunt Yvonne is taking good care of the both of you. Please mind her and help her by being mindful of the manners we have taught you. Soon, Lieblings, darlings, soon we will be together again to see our way through this ugly war. Papa and I love you very much.

Mama and Papa were alive—Rosie felt as if a huge weight had lifted. They were alive—and at Fort Armstrong, whatever and wherever that was! Of course they loved her and Freddie, Rosie had never doubted that for a minute. She sat quietly, clutching the scrap of paper and letting Mama's words warm her. She felt almost weak with the relief of knowing where they were and that someone was working to free them.

"Can we visit them? Will you take a letter back to Mama?" she asked the visitor.

"I cannot return," Mrs. Launius's voice broke. "I am on parole and cannot take the chance to return to the place I was interned."

Rosie glanced at Aunt Yvonne whose lips were pressed tightly together. "Don't you have something to say to Mrs. Launius?" she prompted Rosie.

"Thank you very, very much, Mrs. Launius. It's the best present of all to have word from our mama and papa. I don't even have enough words to tell you how good it is to know that they are alive and well," said Rosie, feeling every word of gratefulness. "And if you'll excuse me, I'd like to share the note with Freddie?" She looked to her aunt for permission.

"Of course." Aunt Yvonne waved Rosie out of the room.

Rosie would share the note with her brother, but not until bedtime. For now it was all hers. Lately, it had been difficult for her and Freddie to sleep, and hearing news of Mama and Papa might help the both of them. She sat on the bed and touched the note. Mama had also touched the paper and written the words on it. Rosie kissed it. She laid it back down and smoothed the wrinkles and folds.

In the hallway, she heard Rainer heading toward his room. Aunt Yvonne would never agree, but perhaps there was a way to convince her cousin to take her to Fort Armstrong.

Rosie pushed open his door and leaned against it before he could slam it shut and turn on his radio—which had not been taken from her aunt's house even though she was as German as Mama—so loud that it would be impossible for him to hear her.

"What?" he asked grumpily.

"I need a favor," Rosie said.

"No." Rainer turned his back and tried to close the door but Rosie blocked it.

"I want you to drive me to Fort Armstrong . . ."

"Where the hell is Fort Armstrong?"

"We can find that out as well. It's where my mother and father are," she added.

"The answer is still no," Rainer said.

"Do you really not care if I tell your mother about Lily?

It might be an accident that I ask whether Rainer's girlfriend will be coming over during the holidays, but I'm sure it will bring up questions."

"And do you really want to be sent to an orphanage?"

Rosie folded her arms and waited. Her cousin couldn't scare her with that. She had made her threat and she was willing to carry it out to make Rainer do what she wanted. Her aunt would die if she knew Rainer was dating a Hawaiian girl.

"I can't show up someplace where Germans are interned," Rainer said flatly.

"You can wait in the car," Rosie countered.

"Mother is afraid we are under surveillance by the FBI and warned me to be careful. I don't think going to check on German internees is being careful. I can't do it."

Her cousin sounded like he was being honest for once. But Rosie wasn't willing to let Rainer off so easily.

"What if it was your parents or your mother who was interned?" she said.

"That sounds pretty damn good to me," said Rainer, smirking.

"Okay." Rosie shrugged. "I never could keep a secret." She turned away, disappointed yet hopeful. Rainer could still change his mind. She walked away slowly.

At her bedroom door, Rainer grabbed her arm. Rosie stifled her smile of triumph and turned, pulling her arm away.

"When? When do you want to go?" he asked. "I hope it isn't on the other side of the island."

"I'll be ready whenever you are," said Rosie.

Chapter 16

Rosie's wait for Rainer to drive her to Fort Armstrong stretched into several days. First, he said he had to find out where the Fort was located.

Rosie took care of that when she finally convinced a reluctant Aunt Yvonne to take her and Freddie to the public library. Rosie was thrilled to have new books to read, but she also searched out an Oahu map with Fort Armstrong clearly marked. She made a sketch of how to drive there in her stolen journal.

Then, Rainer said he had to figure out an excuse to take Rosie in the car with him, and that turned out to be to help him buy a gift for his mother for Christmas. And finally, Rainer had to wait for a chance to borrow his mother's car.

Rosie sat on the edge of the car seat, staring out the windshield. She hadn't seen anything but Aunt Yvonne's house since her trip downtown the week before to her father's radio shop.

Rosie tried to take in all the changes that had occurred because of the war. There were camouflage nets that looked like a strange kind of plant covering various buildings. These must be the nets Kam said his Auntie and her friends were weaving instead of leis. From the number of nets hanging everywhere, they had been very busy.

Even more of the buildings had sandbags piled in front of them, to absorb bomb blasts Rainer said. Fortunately, there had been no further bombs since December 7.

Rosie saw lots of soldiers, and everyone carried a gas mask. But despite the war, the sky was a clear blue, flowers bloomed, and except for the soldiers, people still wore their bright muu-muus and flowered shirts.

Rosie had found out in her research that Fort Armstrong wasn't really a fort but an immigration—I-M-M-I-G-R-A-T-I-O-N—station. There was no mention anyplace Rosie could find that they were keeping the "enemy aliens" they had arrested there.

The "fort" was located on the water. It was the first time Rosie had seen the ocean since the bombing. She breathed in the salty, fishy smell that she loved and realized how much she had missed her family's regular visits to the beach. Papa often said it was his dream to live on the water and now it seemed he had his wish. She hoped they at least had a view.

Rainer pulled up and parked the car outside the station,

but Rosie was suddenly not so sure she wanted to go inside. The building itself wasn't awfully scary. It didn't look how she had pictured a fort but rather it was several low buildings. The scary part was the tall fence that surrounded the buildings and the soldiers holding guns who guarded the buildings.

Rainer had to practically push her out of the car. She smoothed her hair and then her dress. Her shoes felt tight and hot on her feet.

You can fight this fear for Mama and Papa, Rosie thought as she slowly walked down a pavement path leading to the gate marked by a big No Trespassing sign. A very young soldier came slowly toward her, his gun across his chest. Rosie froze.

"The sign says NO TRESPASSING," the soldier said in a voice that broke both high and low.

"I've come to visit my parents, Greta and Henry Schatzer," Rosie said as evenly as she could manage.

"Umm," the soldier managed to say. He looked over his shoulder and walked backward, his eyes still on Rosie. "I need to see . . ." He turned and walked more quickly to another soldier standing in front of the door. The two of them talked in voices too low for her to hear.

Rosie tapped her toe, examined her fingernails (they needed to be trimmed), ran her fingers through her hair, and then patted it back down. The soldiers continued to talk.

Finally, the young one returned. "You can't come in," he said.

"But my mama and papa—" Rosie started.

He shook his head. "No one can come in. I'm—" he stared at the pavement, "I'm sorry."

"I came a long way," Rosie continued.

The soldier shook his head and blocked the gate.

"Please," she tried.

He sighed. "I can't. I just can't. Please go and don't start any trouble."

Rosie turned toward the car and then whirled back to the gate. If she made enough trouble . . . She took one step toward the gate, then another.

"Seriously," the young man said, looking nervously over his shoulder. "It's just a bunch of enemy aliens they're keeping locked up there. I mean, that has nothing to do with you."

Not me, Rosie thought, *and not my parents either.*

She felt tears sting the back of her eyes. She hated that ugly label, enemy alien.

"I don't know where your parents are, but I doubt they are there." He stuck his thumb over his shoulder, pointing toward the fort.

Rosie had been so sure today was the day she'd see Mama and Papa. No matter how much the tears burned, they refused to fall, only blurring her vision and giving her a headache. She turned on her heel and climbed into the waiting car. She felt like she had lost this battle.

"That was a short visit," Rainer said.

"You saw they wouldn't let me inside," she said in clipped tones. *Enemy alien, enemy alien, enemy alien.* The phrase stuck in her mind and wouldn't go away. She leaned against the side window and stared at the fence separating her and the cold, stark building rising before her.

"Bad information, huh?" said Rainer.

Rosie shrugged. She'd been so happy when she'd finally known where her parents were but now she was back to the beginning, wondering and worrying about them. Were they truly being held behind that fence?

Chapter 17

"Anyplace else you want to go?" Rainer asked. "I hate to waste an afternoon with the car."

Rainer almost sounded nice for a change. "Would you drive me back to my house? I want to check on Kitty and maybe pack up more clothes for Freddie and me." Aunt Yvonne always told her not to worry about the cat, but Rosie wanted to check for herself. She pleated the skirt of her dress as she asked, figuring there was little to no chance her cousin would actually take her where she wanted to go.

Rainer started the car and soon Rosie recognized the road to home, at least the place that used to be home.

"It's that one, isn't it?" Rainer asked, signaling his turn.

Rosie leaned forward and drank in first the sight of home, then searched the yard with grass grown ragged for Kitty.

Opening the car door as soon as Rainer pulled to a stop, she called for her cat. There was no answer.

She stared at the house, and the longer Rosie looked at it, the more a feeling of uneasiness crept over her. Besides the uncared-for lawn, she took in the kitchen screen door hanging crookedly off its hinges, a shattered window on the second floor, and one of the kindergarten chairs lying broken on the porch.

Rosie slowly approached the house and uncovered the key she had hidden on a ledge under the porch. She also quickly checked the darkness underneath for a sign of Kitty, with no luck. And Kitty's dishes she'd left on the porch—where were they?

Rosie moved more quickly. She inserted the key into the lock but before she could turn it, the door swung open.

"What you doing here?" a voice demanded.

Rosie stepped back, almost tripping over her own feet. Malia! What was a teacher from the kindergarten doing here?

"Rosie?" Malia asked, scowling.

"What are you doing here?" the two of them asked in unison.

"I came to pick up some clothes and some of our other things," Rosie explained, trying to see around Malia.

"This is my house now," Malia declared.

"No," Rosie said. "No!" she repeated more forcefully.

"I will reopen *my* nursery again," Malia said. "And run it *my* way."

Rosie shook her head. "But you can't! This is our house."

"Not anymore. And look what I have to do before I can have the *keiki*. No more *kinder*, no more Nazi." Malia moved aside and pulled Rosie into the kitchen.

Rosie gasped. The cupboard doors hung open to empty shelves. The room had been emptied of furniture although debris—D-E-B-R-I-S, she spelled nervously—littered the space.

Ignoring Malia, Rosie raced up the stairs to her room. The bookshelves were overturned and random papers with ragged edges were spread about the floor. All the other furniture was gone and the closet door had been removed. Everything that had been inside the closet was also gone. And her journal. It was all gone.

Rosie wandered more slowly through Freddie's room—empty; the guest room—empty; the living room—bare; Mama's and Papa's room. All had been vandalized. V-A-N-D-A-L-I-Z-E-D! The quilts were gone, Mama's jewelry box, toys from Freddie's room, even the curtains were torn from the windows.

Rosie turned and almost ran into Malia, unaware the woman had followed her. "Did you do this? Where are our things?"

"Me? Why I want your things? The man who sold me the house said they had been put in storage. After that, who knows? Leave a house empty these days and it will end up like this one."

"Sold? That isn't right. No one could sell you this house."

"I have the papers," Malia said. "Now, you go." She pointed down the stairs.

"Who is this man who said our things were in storage?" Rosie asked.

"His name Mr. Smith." Malia put her hand on Rosie's back and pushed her gently toward the staircase.

Rosie looked at the bare walls, the empty rooms as she passed by. Outside on the porch, she looked up at the sky. How could she feel so cold when the sun shone so brightly?

"Got what you need?" Rainer called.

Rosie shook her head. "It's gone," she managed to say as she joined her cousin. "Everything." She searched the yard again. "Even Kitty."

Rainer jumped up on the porch and looked in the open door. "Hello," he said, "who are you?" Even her cousin looked shocked at the state of the house and the appearance of a strange woman.

"Out!" Malia said firmly. "This is my house, my school now. I pay good money for it. Go! Go!"

Rainer backed away. "Looks like," he said, "well, we'd better go!"

"One more thing," Rosie said, summoning the nerve to ask about her cat.

"No more thing!" Malia said and she slammed the door shut.

Perhaps, Rosie thought as she returned to the car, if Kitty hadn't come at the sound of her voice, the cat had already forgotten her.

Chapter 18

"Just go . . ." Rosie started to say "back to Aunt Yvonne's," but stopped. "No, turn in at the next driveway." She looked back at her former home and noticed a sign in the yard:

COMING SOON!

ISLAND NURSERY

NEW TEACHERS

ALL HAWAIIAN

Rosie was surprised Malia hadn't added "No Nazis," considering her earlier words. And their home sold? She couldn't believe Mama and Papa had agreed to that.

There were children playing in Auntie Palu's yard, and for a moment it seemed like life as it had always been.

Before she was out of the car, Auntie Palu stepped off her porch, so much like the one at Rosie's house, and shaded her eyes, staring. Rosie waved.

"Roselie! My Roselie!" Auntie Palu said, clapping her hands and hurrying toward her. She enveloped Rosie in a warm hug, the warmest she had enjoyed since her Aunt Etta had been taken away.

"What happened to you? Where you go? Your family, poof! It goes away like that," said Auntie Palu, still holding Rosie close.

"The government men, they came and took Mama, and Papa too, from work. Then they took Aunt Etta when she came to stay with us and we had to go to Aunt Yvonne's and now Malia . . ." Rosie's words ran together as they rushed from her mouth. "She says our house is hers! And someone took all of our things from the house. Our clothes, my books, every-thing!"

"Shh! Shh!" Auntie Palu rocked her gently. "Why did you not come to stay with Auntie Palu?"

"We came and knocked on the door. No one was home!" Rosie told her.

Auntie's forehead creased. "When was that? The day after the bombing? Ah! I went with my boys to sign up for the ser-vice. Leilani and I stayed to serve the other boys—my Rosie, they are only small boys! I spread aloha spirit to them and decided that will be my war work. To make sure our boys leave Hawaii brimming with aloha spirit. I believe that will protect them from evil.

"We miss our good neighbors, the Schatzers. And we have tried to keep the bad people away from your house. But there are too many and we are sorry, so sorry we could not protect your home." Auntie Palu hugged Rosie again. "But this Malia, I did not know about this."

"She is reopening the kindergarten, only she calls it hers. And she said she bought the house. That can't be!"

"Your papa will have something to say about that!" Auntie Palu said.

"But Papa . . ." Rosie started.

"Leilani!" Auntie Palu called. "See who has shown up to visit us!"

"Hi," Rosie greeted her friend shyly when she stepped out onto the porch. Rosie wasn't sure if Leilani was still mad at her.

"Hi," Leilani returned, not smiling. But at least she was speaking.

"You must lend Rosie a few things to wear until she can buy new. And some things for Freddie, too. You two, go along and gather while I put together some dishes of food for Rosie and her Auntie Yvonne."

Leilani looked Rosie up and down. "We don't really wear the same kind of clothes," she said.

"Anything will be better than the two dresses I currently have!" Rosie said, trying to be funny.

"I'm sorry my clothes don't come up to your high standards." Leilani turned and climbed the stairs with Rosie following behind her.

"I didn't mean it that way!" Rosie said. "I was joking. Seriously, all I have are two dresses that I packed, thinking we would be back in a couple of days. And now it's been over two weeks! Freddie doesn't even have shoes."

"You won't be able to wear anything of mine to that fancy school you plan to go to," Leilani said, rummaging through her drawers.

"You mean Punahou? I've hardly thought about that since I've been gone. I mean, I have more important things. My parents are gone! Didn't you receive my letter?" Rosie had hoped her friend would have some ideas about what they could do to find out about Mama and Papa. But this girl didn't seem to be the friend she remembered.

"No letter," Leilani said with a shrug. "Wait here while I go find some things for Freddie," she said, not responding with even one word of sympathy or comfort to what Rosie had said about her parents.

Rosie sat down on Leilani's bed. Her aunt hadn't mailed the letter after all. And Leilani was still mad. She picked up a book, open on the pillow. It was a Nancy Drew, one of the same ones Rosie had read and reread at Aunt Yvonne's. A second book stuck out from underneath the pillow. Rosie pulled it out and stared.

Rosie recognized the spelling guide that George had brought her from the newspaper office. She opened it to the first page and the words seemed to leap off the page: "Good luck, Champ! Love, George"

Leilani grabbed the book out of her hand.

"That's mine. It was in my room. How did you . . ." Rosie said.

"You weren't using it," Leilani said, her back turned to Rosie. "I only borrowed it."

Rosie wasn't sure what to say. She felt . . . betrayed. Leilani had been in her house since they had gone and she had taken at least the spelling guide. Auntie Palu did not know about this, Rosie was sure.

Leilani disappeared into the hallway with the book.

Rosie waited a moment, then returned to the kitchen. Would she and Leilani ever be friends again? A lump formed in Rosie's throat, and she felt it squeezing its way upwards toward her eyes. She swallowed once, twice, and it was gone—leaving only a bitter taste in her mouth.

"Call that cousin of yours in here," Auntie Palu said. "You must have a snack before you go back. You are thin, so thin!"

"Rainer . . . has more errands to run," Rosie said, wanting to leave before Leilani came downstairs, even if it meant leaving the borrowed clothes behind. "But one more question. Kitty?"

"Not here. But I will watch for her. Cats, they take care of themselves, dearie. She will be fine. And you will be fine, too. You will be back with your mama and papa and we will celebrate your homecoming!" Auntie Palu piled Rosie's arms with containers of food.

The food smelled delicious. So different from what she ate at Aunt Yvonne's. Rosie smiled as best she could. "Thank you. I'll try to come back and visit as soon as I can."

"Do you have the things I asked Leilani to gather?"

Rosie shook her head.

"Leilani! Where are you? Rosie must leave!"

Leilani dropped a bag at Rosie's feet and turned to go without a word.

"Can't you see she has full arms? Help her!" Auntie Palu scolded.

Leilani sighed and picked up the bag.

Rosie led the way to the car, neither of them speaking.

"Rainer, open the back door please. Auntie Palu is sending all this food home with us," said Rosie.

"What? She thinks we aren't feeding you?" He scrambled out of the driver's seat, straightening his shoulders and grinning when Leilani joined him on his side of the car.

"So, who are you?" Rainer asked.

"That's just Leilani. You've met her before," Rosie said as Leilani smiled at Rainer in a way Rosie didn't like.

"I hope you are coming to Punahou with my cousin," Rainer said, leaning close to Leilani.

Leilani tossed the bag of clothing into the car, glared at Rosie, then said, "I wouldn't be caught dead in that snooty school." She stalked off without even a glance behind her.

Chapter 19

Rosie felt defeated. She had no home if Malia was to be believed. She had no best friend. Worst of all she hadn't been able to see her parents. And she still had to go with Rainer while he picked out a gift for his mother.

Rainer insisted she come out of the car and shop with him. Rosie walked slightly behind her cousin, uninterested even in window decorations. She heard a familiar voice calling to her and turned to see her friend Mollie waving at her.

The girls ran to one another and hugged tightly. "I love this extra-long Christmas vacation, how about you?" Mollie asked.

"Except for the reason we're having it, I like it pretty much," Rosie said weakly.

"Have you heard from Punahou yet? I haven't told anyone that you applied, just like you asked," Mollie said. Mollie also hoped to go to the school, she had confided when she overheard Rosie in the school office requesting that her records be sent to Punahou. "I haven't heard a thing and we might not hear at all. Mother said the military had taken over the campus. Can you imagine?"

Nothing the military did surprised Rosie at this point, but she pretended to be shocked at the idea. "My word!" she said.

"So, what are you getting for Christmas?" Mollie asked. "I'm shopping for my—ugh!—bratty little brother. Mother is making me."

"I don't know really," Rosie said, staring at her foot as she moved it back and forth on the walkway.

"Mollie!" a voice called sharply.

"Mother! It's Rosie Schatzer! She hasn't heard from Punahou either."

"And I doubt she will," Mollie's mother said. "Get back here!"

"Guess I have to go. Maybe we can get together sometime before we go back to . . ."

"Mollie, I said now."

Mollie shook her head and ran back to her mother. The woman grabbed her daughter's shoulder and leaned close to her face, talking, then looking at Rosie, then talking again. She grabbed Mollie's hand and pulled her the opposite direction from Rosie. Mollie looked back, a strange expression on her face.

Rosie's face burned. They knew about her parents! She

couldn't read lips but their actions and expressions said as much as words could—with Mollie's mother's disapproving and Mollie's shocked. She suspected that Mollie would not be calling her. Did everyone know?

Rosie suddenly felt like everyone was looking at her, that everyone knew her parents were accused of doing awful things that they would never do in a million years. But that was the part no one ever thought about. The fact they were locked up automatically made them guilty and her, too, by association—A-S-S-O-C-I-A-T-I-O-N. If others knew of her German background, they might think she, too, was an "enemy alien" or worse, a Nazi.

"Got it!" Rainer held up a wrapped gift. "No thanks to you."

"I'm ready to go back," Rosie said.

"Thought we might find a place and have a cold soda," Rainer said, pointing at a café nearby.

Rosie shook her head, pulling at her hair to cover her face.

"You ruin everything! I have the car and all you want to do is go home. I hope Mom sees the light after Christmas and sends the two of you where you belong."

Rainer slammed the door so hard the car shook. Rosie scrunched down in the seat. She couldn't bear everyone looking at her and wondering what her parents had done. Aunt Yvonne was right. They should stay close to the house and not talk to anyone.

Chapter 20

"Rosie! Wake up," Freddie bounced up and down on the bed. "I can't find my clothes!"

Waking up to that news did not improve Rosie's mood. She was still trying to recover from the day before, which had felt like one of her worst ever.

Their clothes *were* gone and Rosie decided someone, probably Aunt Yvonne, had taken them to be washed. The only clothes left in the room were in the bag that Leilani had put together for them. And the feeling Rosie had gotten from her one-time best friend did not bode well for what the bag contained.

Rosie dumped the contents onto the bed and started to go through it.

There were sandals for Freddie. "Aunt Yvonne will be happy about these," he said as he tossed them to the floor.

Separating the clothes into two piles for her and her brother, Rosie paused when she came upon a flowered dress with a full skirt. It had always been one of Leilani's dresses that she liked best. Also in the jumble, Rosie found a yellow top with blue flowers, another favorite, and a sky blue gathered skirt that she had also always liked. These were some of Leilani's best clothes! And she had passed them along. Now, Rosie felt even more confused. This generosity—G-E-N-E-R-O-S-I-T-Y—on Leilani's part contradicted her words and actions from yesterday!

And underneath all the clothing was the spelling guide. Rosie could only stare at it.

Freddie grabbed the first two items of clothing he could reach and rushed outside to meet up with his new friend, Rex. The two of them had amassed a collection of metal pieces and parts they claimed came from bomb damage. They had to leave it in Rex's yard because Aunt Yvonne didn't want it messing up hers. Rosie envied the fact that Freddie had someone to play with.

Rosie dressed in the skirt and top, wanting to save the dress for a more special occasion. They fit almost perfectly, which meant that Leilani had probably outgrown them. Still, she chose something she knew Rosie liked. That had to mean something.

Rosie wanted breakfast even if Freddie would rather play. She went downstairs to see if Kealani was around. Sometimes she brought treats she or her mother had cooked and they were a welcome break from Aunt Yvonne's cooking. Or, she might finish off some of the cookies Auntie Palu had sent. Last night her aunt had served something new and different—beans and a canned meat she'd called Spam. It tasted pretty bad and Rosie was extra hungry today. Her mother would never serve such a thing, although Aunt Yvonne claimed she had no choice as it was harder and harder to find fresh food.

Kealani looked up from where she was standing at the sink. "Aloha," she said quietly.

"Hi," said Rosie. "Is there any breakfast left?" she asked hopefully.

"I brought some things from our early Christmas luau," Kealani said. "My brothers have gone to the Army and yet, we cook as if they still live with us!" She laughed. "But I will fix you a delicious snack."

"You go ahead with what you are doing," Rosie said. "I can fix my own." Rosie removed containers from the refrigerator that smelled so good they made her mouth water.

"And there's something else for you," said Kealani, handing Rosie a folded square of fabric.

Rosie laid the food aside and took the square to the table. She slowly unfolded it. The square was a soft ivory with a green cutout piece basted to it. Rosie traced the shape carefully with her finger—it was a circle of fish.

"I will teach you to quilt, then I will teach you how to make your own pattern," said Kealani. "This pattern, I make for you with aloha spirit." She smiled shyly.

"It is beautiful," Rosie whispered.

"It will take you time to quilt it. First we applique. When we finish, your mama and papa will have returned. I am sure of it with my very breath. I put many prayers into the pattern."

"You are so kind." Rosie picked up the quilt square and examined it. "I hope—I don't know if I can . . . I've never even held a needle. Auntie Palu said when she finished teaching Mama, she would start on me, but Mama was still learning."

"You will do fine. Eat and we will begin. The quilting will fill you with aloha spirit."

Rosie practically inhaled her breakfast, while watching Kealani thread a needle with green thread the same shade as the cutout pattern. When Rosie finished, Kealani moved closer to her and showed her how to turn the edges of the cutout under and secure it with tiny green stitches.

Rosie stayed at the kitchen table while Kealani worked around her, washing dishes, cooking, and cleaning the floor. She bent close to the fabric and with each stitch felt a little hope that her parents would soon return. Aloha spirit would bring them back, and she would make sure to sew only positive thoughts about their homecoming into the square.

When she finally straightened up, Rosie's eyes and shoulders ached. She stretched and blinked, looking across the room where everything appeared blurry. She blinked more and stood, stretching more. Folding the square, she thanked Kealani and then headed to the bedroom to write in her journal for a while.

Kealani is right that quilting does something to quiet the spirit. After working on the quilt today, I feel much better. Because yesterday was one of my worst days ever. First Leilani, who I worry that things will never be the same with again. After seeing the clothes she sent me, I am hopeful I am wrong about that. Maybe Auntie Palu is right and Leilani is confused. I have to find a way to talk to her and set everything right. For now, she is one more thing that makes the world seem off balance.

Then Mollie. We were happy to see one another until her mother pulled her away and spoke to her. I hope this isn't a sample of what is to come when I return to school. I felt very rejected.

But worst of all, we don't have a home to return to if what Malia said is true. That our house is now hers. I told Aunt Yvonne what Malia had said and she said she would mention it to Uncle Charles. That's it. That's all she said. I told her there was a man Malia said was named Mr. Smith and that we should try to find him and talk to him. Aunt Yvonne again said she would tell Uncle Charles. We have barely seen Uncle Charles since we came here so I think he is too busy to take on another job.

And I still haven't seen my mama and papa or Aunt Etta.

What would Nancy Drew do?

A loud knock on the front door made Rosie's pencil skitter across the page. She waited to see if she needed to go downstairs and answer. She set the spiral notebook and pencil aside and scooted toward the edge of the bed when she heard Aunt Yvonne open the door. She constantly hoped the next knock would be Mama and Papa.

It wasn't. Rosie heard her aunt talking with a man whose voice she didn't recognize.

Very quietly, Rosie crept to the top of the staircase and peered over the railing. A short man, very round and red-faced, stood on the blue flowered rug holding a stack of gifts. The man reminded her of Santa.

Rosie strained to hear what her aunt and the man said.

". . . Mrs. Schatzer's sister?" the man said.

Aunt Yvonne nodded and said something Rosie couldn't make out.

". . . at the house. . . . parents bought for the children before they were arrested," the man said.

"And how do you happen to have them?" Aunt Yvonne said.

". . . enemy aliens . . . property," she heard of his response.

Was this the mysterious Mr. Smith Malia had mentioned the day before? The one who was dealing with their property? Rosie waited to hear more, although she knew Nancy Drew would jump right in. But Nancy didn't have to constantly deal with Aunt Yvonne and her rules.

The gifts were like a magnet and kept claiming her attention. There were two rectangular-shaped gifts on top, two medium-sized, squishy-looking gifts each wrapped in different paper, and one large gift on the very bottom. Could they truly be for her and Freddie? She was sure she'd heard the man say "parents bought for the children before they were arrested." And who else in this house had parents who were arrested?

The sight of the gaily wrapped gifts sent a wave of holiday cheer washing over Rosie. Santa! Presents! Mama and Papa had managed somehow to send them presents.

Aunt Yvonne took the stack from the man and the two top presents slid off. Her aunt spoke to the man, calling him Mr. Smith, and confirming Rosie's suspicion. It was strange how someone who had taken so much from them looked like Santa Claus.

As her aunt scolded Mr. Smith, Rosie had to smile—even Santa wasn't immune from being told off by her aunt. Mr. Smith quickly picked up the dropped gifts and offered to carry them for Aunt Yvonne. She handed them over and directed him toward the back of the house.

Rosie started down the stairs.

"And what do you think you are doing, Miss Priss?" Aunt Yvonne said as she returned to the hall and looked up at Rosie.

Her aunt made her feel like she'd been caught doing something she shouldn't. "Who is that man?" Rosie asked. "Is he here about my parents? Did you ask him about our house?" Why did her aunt have to see her before she had a chance to confront Mr. Smith?

"Your parents? Why would you think that? What he is here for is no concern of yours. Let's say it is a Christmas miracle and leave it be. Go back to whatever you were doing."

A Christmas miracle would be my parents returning, Rosie thought.

"Rosie," her aunt said, a warning in her voice.

Rosie heard a car engine and ran the rest of the way down the stairs to the front door. She pulled it open and a dark car was backing into the street.

"He's gone!" She turned to her aunt angrily.

Aunt Yvonne returned her angry look with one of her own and disappeared into the hallway.

Rosie stomped back the way she had come, vowing to find Mr. Smith to learn for herself what he knew about her parents.

Chapter 21

On Christmas day, Freddie woke Rosie up. "Do you think Santa knows we're here?" he asked.

"Freddie, I'm pretty sure that Santa knows where everyone is," Rosie said, stretching and yawning. For the past two days since she'd seen Mr. Smith delivering gifts, she had imagined and wondered what was inside those cheery holiday boxes, and today she would finally find out!

Before Rosie could tell him to get up quietly, her brother slid out of bed and ran into the hall.

"Rosie! There are presents!" he shouted.

Rosie wasn't sure what they should do. Wait for Aunt Yvonne? In the bedroom? Downstairs? If they were home, she and Freddie would run into Mama and Papa's room, jump on the bed, and wake them. They would pretend to not want to wake up but Rosie and Freddie would pull them out of the bed anyway, everyone laughing. Rosie thought this should be a happy memory but it made her very sad.

"You children are up early," Uncle Charles's voice came from the hallway. Rosie had barely seen her uncle since they'd moved in as he worked constantly. She hoped he'd be able to stay home with them today. Perhaps she would have a chance to ask him questions about her parents. Besides, Uncle Charles was more fun than Aunt Yvonne!

"Presents!" Freddie said.

Aunt Yvonne called out from the bedroom but Rosie couldn't make out what she'd said.

Uncle Charles clapped his hands together. "Get dressed and wait for me and Aunt Yvonne in the living room."

Rosie finally pushed the covers off and stood up, stretching. She'd wear Leilani's special dress today in honor of the holiday.

Freddie rushed in and tore off his pajamas and slipped into the same shorts and shirt he always wore, nothing special at all.

As Rosie started to leave the bedroom, she realized they had no gifts for her aunt and uncle. In fact, she hadn't even thought of buying them anything. How could she? What could she? "Freddie," she whispered as he tried to push past her, "we don't have anything for Aunt Yvonne and Uncle Charles."

Freddie shrugged. "Santa probably brought them something too."

Rosie tried to think of something they could make—quickly—with supplies they had.

"We could pick some flowers," Freddie suggested.

"Aunt Yvonne would kill us," said Rosie.

"Yeah, she would," Freddie agreed.

"I know! We can make them breakfast. Pancakes. I know how to cook pancakes and you can help me," Rosie said, knowing it wasn't the best present ever but it would be something.

"After we open our presents?" Freddie asked.

"Let's go start right now. You know how long it takes Aunt Yvonne . . ." Before she could finish, Freddie grabbed her hand and started down the stairs.

"See!" He pointed to two presents stacked on the table in the living room.

"I see." Rosie started toward the kitchen, then turned back. There were only two gifts on the table from the pile she'd seen Mr. Smith bring. The two small square packages and the very large present were missing! Had she been wrong? Rosie tried not to let it worry her.

She continued to the kitchen, urging Freddie to follow her.

She opened cabinets and pulled out ingredients, thankful to find a box of pancake mix that was almost full. "You set the table in the dining room," she told Freddie.

Rosie tried to be careful as she added milk and eggs to the mix, but some of the flour spilled on the kitchen table and one of the eggs dripped. She decided it was more important to finish her preparations than to clean up as she went along. There would be time for that later. While the pancakes cooked in

Aunt Yvonne's black frying pan, Rosie found syrup and butter and called Freddie to come get them as well.

She'd cooked two skillets of nice round cakes with only the first one coming out poorly when Aunt Yvonne arrived.

"What are you doing!" her aunt asked, standing in the doorway looking horrified. "Don't you know it is dangerous for children to use the stove? And this mess!" She pointed to the table.

"It's our present for you and Uncle Charles," Rosie said quietly, rethinking her idea as she took in her aunt's reaction.

"Isn't that thoughtful?" Uncle Charles placed his hands on Aunt Yvonne's shoulders and turned her away from the kitchen.

"I'll clean up, too. That's another part of the gift," Rosie said. Her mama and papa loved it when she made them pancakes. What were they doing today? Would they have a chance to celebrate?

"Thank you," Uncle Charles said over his shoulder, smiling broadly. "It's very nice of you."

Rosie brought in the platter of pancakes and Aunt Yvonne took one. Uncle Charles covered his plate with pancakes and Freddie took the rest.

"A little cold—" Aunt Yvonne said before Uncle Charles interrupted.

"Yum! Best pancakes I've had in ages. Maybe we should turn the cooking over to Rosie and Freddie."

Rosie let Uncle Charles's words warm her.

"Hmph!" Aunt Yvonne ate another tiny bite. "Where's Rainer?" she asked, looking around suddenly.

"Still in bed, I'm willing to bet," Uncle Charles said, his mouth full as he shoveled in another forkful of pancakes dripping with syrup.

Rosie cooked one more batch, mostly for herself, and joined the family at the table. She thought the pancakes were just right and ate three.

Freddie's fork clattered on his plate. "I'm done," he said and looked over his shoulder into the living room.

"Let me clear the table," Rosie said. "If you help, it will go faster," she said to Freddie. Freddie sighed loudly and tagged along behind her.

"Darling," Aunt Yvonne said to Uncle Charles. Rosie knew that was who she was talking to because she had never called her or Freddie darling. "Coffee, please."

Uncle Charles picked up his plate and Aunt Yvonne's and carried them into the kitchen. "Thank you," he said to Rosie as she wiped down the kitchen table and made sure she had put everything away in its place. "That was a wonderful present." He squeezed her shoulders. "Wait until after we open presents to finish in here. Freddie is about to blow a gasket."

"I'm glad you're home today," Rosie said.

"Just for a while," Uncle Charles answered. "I'll go in to work later."

"On Christmas Day!"

"War doesn't take holidays," he replied solemnly.

Rosie had no idea what her uncle even did for work, but she figured it must be important.

"Our parents coming home is the only present I really want," she admitted quietly.

"Ah, yes. We are working on that and wish we could do more." Uncle Charles patted her shoulder again. "And Rosie, try to be patient with your aunt. She has very bad memories of what it meant to be German in the last war. She and your mother were left out and cut out by people they considered their friends. Their father's income suffered because no one wanted to do business with Germans." Uncle Charles shook his head. "She is worried the same thing will happen again and it will affect me and Rainer."

It has *happened*, Rosie thought. It affected her and Freddie and Mama and Papa. Aunt Yvonne was still living her same life. Uncle Charles's words did explain why Mama had grown so frightened when the bombing started, though—she feared what might be coming again.

"Let me tell you a story Yvonne told me. She and Greta attended a local dance, at one of the other sugar plantations at the beginning of the first war with the Germans. The music started playing and boys asked one girl after another to dance until everyone except your mother and your aunt was on the floor whirling around. The entire evening passed and not one boy asked them to dance. They finally left and Yvonne said they felt humiliated—they were ignored because they were German. After that, until the war was over and the prejudices died down, your aunt, and your mama, too, were very careful where they went and who they associated with."

Rosie nodded. She wished Mama had talked about those experiences. They might help her understand what was happening now.

"Does that help you understand your aunt better?"

Rosie tried hard to understand Aunt Yvonne's nervousness, her fears. But she couldn't figure out why her aunt seemed to take all her bad feelings out on her and Freddie. They must remind her of Mama and the bad times they experienced together.

"Be patient?" Uncle Charles repeated as he poured two cups of coffee, adding milk and sugar to one.

"Sure." Rosie smiled as she followed her uncle into the living room, trying to think Christmasy thoughts.

Freddie had placed his gift beside him on the sofa and hers on the neighboring cushion. "Here! Rosie, this is yours!" He practically danced with excitement.

"You may open," Aunt Yvonne said.

Freddie tore the paper off his one present before Rosie could even lift hers.

Freddie held up a pair of pajamas and stared down at the underwear resting in the wrapping paper. He looked at Rosie and she saw tears glistening in his eyes.

"You needed pajamas. Now maybe you won't keep pulling the blanket off me at night," she said as she quickly unwrapped her gift, also pajamas and underwear. Rosie felt slightly embarrassed for Uncle Charles to see such personal items of her clothing. But the embarrassment was overwhelmed by disappointment. Pajamas and underwear! Where were the real gifts? She looked around.

"What was Santa thinking?" Freddie said to Rosie.

"Probably that there is a war going on," Aunt Yvonne said. "You are very fortunate to have these nice gifts. There are some children who have nothing and will receive nothing because of the war."

Aunt Yvonne certainly knew how to put a damper on holiday cheer. "I think I'll do the dishes now," said Rosie, wanting to be alone. She missed her parents more than ever, her chest actually ached with wanting to see them. And she couldn't stop thinking about those other presents the man had delivered, the ones he had said were from her parents. Would Aunt Yvonne have put the gifts away someplace and not let her and Freddie have them because they weren't needy enough? Did she donate them to other children? Rosie tried to think of that as a good thing.

In the kitchen, Rosie stared out the window over the sink. The day was clear and bright and the flowers glowed like jewels in the sunlight. She stuck her hands into the warm suds.

"The gifts were from your parents," Uncle Charles said, startling Rosie, who hadn't heard him come into the room. "There's a man, Mr. Smith, who is taking care of properties for those . . ." Uncle Charles paused, "interned."

Interned? I-N-T-E-R-N-E-D. Might as well say I-M-P-R-I-S-O-N-E-D. It meant the same thing.

"He went out to your house at your parents' request, and delivered the gifts to us to give to you."

"That was nice," Rosie said. "I guess Mama and Papa didn't have time to buy anything else."

"Next year, Rosie. They will make up for it next year," Uncle Charles said.

She turned to Uncle Charles. "So, this Mr. Smith, how much can he do to Mama and Papa's property? One day Rainer and I drove by the house and someone, Malia, who used to be a teacher at Mama's school, was there. She said she had bought the house and was going to open a nursery school. Can Mr. Smith do that? Did he say anything to Aunt Yvonne about our house? About where all our things were? Our furniture? Our clothes? Kitty? Did he say anything about my cat?" Rosie knew the answer since she had been listening from the steps, but if Uncle Charles knew anything, now would be a good time to find out.

Uncle Charles started shaking his head before Rosie finished. "I'm sorry. After he stopped by here and we finally knew who was handling your parents' property, I gave him a call. He mentioned storage, I think. And he said expenses were mounting and he was trying to find a way to cover them. Taxes, insurance, things you wouldn't be interested in. He mentioned he might have to liquidate some things but I didn't interpret that to mean real estate. I'll check further next week. Promise." He patted her shoulder again as Rosie hung her head. "What I don't understand is why Henry didn't ask me to handle his property."

Perhaps her parents had tried. Aunt Yvonne always said she had no time for one more thing. Managing property might take some of her precious time.

"I think I'll wake up Rainer. He's going to be excited about his gift! A new surfboard. I wish I had time to go to the beach." Uncle Charles turned to leave, then turned back, "*Mele Kalikimaka!*" he said.

"*Froehliche weihnachten,*" Rosie said with a smile.

Uncle Charles frowned and placed a finger over his lips. "No German," he whispered. "Not in these days."

Rosie pressed her lips together. She hated feeling ashamed of being German, but it was coming at her from all sides. Enemy alien. Internment. No German.

Uncle Charles left her standing there, her dishwater cooling.

They hadn't read *A Christmas Carol* or *The Night Before Christmas* or sung even one Christmas carol so far. There was no tree, no lights . . . no idea what might happen next.

Chapter 22

The day after Christmas, Rainer left early for the beach to try his new surfboard. Freddie asked to go along, but Rainer laughed. "Babies don't surf!" he said. "And neither do orphans!"

Instead of tearing up, Freddie rammed his head into Rainer's stomach, slamming the bigger boy backward into a table and knocking a glass bowl to the floor, shattering it.

"What now!" Aunt Yvonne ran down the steps and stood looking at the mess on the floor.

Rosie quickly pushed Freddie behind her. "He didn't mean to break it. Rainer was teasing him."

Rainer rubbed his stomach, then doubled over and groaned. "He gave me a head butt, right in the bread basket," he moaned.

"To your room!" Aunt Yvonne glared at Freddie and pointed upstairs.

Rosie was already on her hands and knees, cleaning the broken glass.

Freddie ran up the steps and Rosie heard the door to their room slam shut. She'd felt like doing the same thing as her brother had to their cousin but had never quite had the nerve. It was almost as much fun to tease him about his girlfriend and whether or not she was going to tell. That was how she'd make him treat her brother a little nicer.

"I have to be gone today. Your uncle wants me to accompany him to a reception at Army headquarters. Hopefully you can keep your brother from destroying anything else," Aunt Yvonne said.

Army headquarters? Rosie's ears perked. If only she had the chance to talk to someone in charge!

"Maybe you could ask about our parents?" Rosie sat back on her heels.

"We shall see if it is appropriate," Aunt Yvonne said and returned upstairs.

A-P-P-R-O-P-R-I-A-T-E. Rosie sat in the hallway, surrounded by shards of glass, without saying a word. Rainer left with his surfboard. His stomach couldn't be that bad if he was still going surfing, she thought. And she and Freddie would enjoy a day at the beach! But . . .

Rosie looked toward the back of the house, where she'd seen the mysterious Mr. Smith and Aunt Yvonne disappear with a stack of presents. And yet a much shorter stack—only two presents—had reappeared. As soon as her aunt left, Rosie intended to search for the missing packages, just like Nancy Drew. She smiled to herself.

"I should be back sometime this afternoon," Aunt Yvonne called from the front door as Rosie threw the remains of the glass bowl in the trash. "Remember what I said!"

A car horn sounded, the front door opened and closed, followed by silence. Rosie relaxed, enjoying being out from under her aunt's scrutiny for the moment. Then she couldn't wait any longer. "Freddie!" she called.

Her brother didn't answer. Rosie called again and when he still didn't answer, she ran up the stairs to bring him down.

Freddie was sprawled across the bed when she opened the door.

"Hey," she greeted him.

"Hay is for horses," he said.

"I may have a surprise," Rosie continued.

"More pajamas? Or better yet, underwear?" her brother said, still not looking at her.

"Yeah, those were pretty bad presents. But," Rosie held her secret to herself for a moment longer, then said, "I think there are some more presents from Mama and Papa."

Freddie lifted his head and looked over his shoulder. "So why didn't Aunt Yvonne give them to us?"

That was the million dollar question in Rosie's mind, too. "Don't know, but why don't you come and help me find them? Like a treasure hunt!"

Slowly, Freddie rose from the bed. "I guess," he said.

"Hey, you're a sourpuss today!"

"Just being like you," said Freddie.

Was she a sourpuss? Rosie thought of how dark the days had seemed since their parents had left and how slowly they passed. Perhaps she had been a sourpuss and perhaps she should try to fix that.

"A man came one day, and he had packages. We opened two of them yesterday but he had more. He and Aunt Yvonne went to the back of the house." Rosie led her brother to the kitchen. She looked around.

"Maybe Aunt Yvonne took them to the orphanist," Freddie said.

Rosie wasn't willing to give in to that idea yet, that her aunt had donated their gifts, although she considered it possible.

"Don't give up yet," said Rosie. "We haven't even looked."

Freddie opened each cabinet, one by one. "Nothing there." He opened the refrigerator. "Yuck!" he said.

Rosie knew what he meant. The sour smell of poi spilled out. Kealani must have left some of her lunch behind. Rosie was no fan of the thick, purple Hawaiian staple although she knew her dislike was considered odd for someone who had lived all her life on the islands.

Freddie slammed the door closed.

"Where else can we look?" Rosie tapped her chin, turning in a circle. "You've gone over every inch of this house. Where would be a good place to hide something?"

"The garage?" Freddie said. "We aren't allowed in the garage." He leaned close to Rosie and spoke in a low voice. "But I've been in there. There's a loft and cabinets and lots of tools."

"If I were you, I'd stay out if Aunt Yvonne said not to go in there," Rosie warned.

"But there might be presents hiding there!" Freddie opened the outside door and stepped through to the garage. Rosie followed.

"I'll climb up in the loft and see if they are there," he said, and like a monkey, he was up the wooden rungs nailed into the wall and onto the loft floor before Rosie had a chance to say a word.

"There's a bicycle! And boxes with baby toys! And boxes with books!" Freddie came to the edge and looked over at Rosie.

The mention of books was all it took for Rosie to climb into the loft. But once up, she also had a bird's-eye view of most of the garage from above and there the presents were! She recognized the gift wrap, shape, and size of them. Her little brother was a better detective than she was.

"Do you think Aunt Yvonne would let me ride the bike?"

"I don't know, but I see the presents." Rosie started to say Mama and Papa had gotten them but remembered her brother still believed in Santa. And he must be very disappointed in the old guy for bringing him clothes. "I think these presents must be from Mama and Papa, or maybe Santa."

"Let's go see!" Freddie swung down off the loft, reaching

for the wooden ladder. Rosie wasn't sure what happened but the next thing she knew her brother was on the cement floor, holding on to his arm, crying loudly.

"My arm! My arm!" Freddie sat up slowly and cradled his left arm against his chest.

When Rosie looked down, she saw red oozing out from between her brother's fingers. "What happened?" she called as she descended, slowly and carefully, and knelt beside Freddie. She could see that something was very wrong.

"Is it just your arm? Do you hurt anywhere else?"

Freddie shook his head. "But my arm . . . I want Mama!" He cried louder.

Rosie gently pried his hand off his arm and took a quick look at the cut underneath. She looked away, feeling her breakfast churn in her stomach. The skin was laid open and the blood continued to almost pump out.

"Sit here, quietly, while I go find a towel or something to wrap around your arm." Rosie scrambled up and into the kitchen. She pulled open a drawer and dug out some towels. Who should she call? She had no idea where Aunt Yvonne had gone and Rainer was at the beach. She'd have to go to a neighbor's house.

Rosie knelt beside Freddie and wrapped a towel around the cut. "What happened?"

"There was something metal, like a sharp knife, and my arm caught on it," Freddie managed to say as his body heaved with sobs. "It hurts! It hurts!"

"You probably need stitches." Rosie wanted to hug Freddie but was afraid she'd hurt him even more.

Freddie shook his head. "It will hurt! NO!" He cried harder and leaned against Rosie, smearing blood on her dress. "Just put a bandage on it."

Rosie patted her brother on his back until he settled. Then, the two of them sat quietly as Rosie tried to figure out what she should do next. She thought there might be a doctor who lived nearby.

"I bet Aunt Yvonne will send us to an orphanist for sure now," Freddie said with a sniff.

"No, shhh! She will be so sad that you are hurt. And we will take good care of you until Mama comes home. Maybe we'll even make haupia."

It hadn't been near long enough for her aunt to be gone, but a car pulled up in the driveway and Rosie heard Aunt Yvonne tell the driver good-bye. She had never felt this glad to see her aunt!

As Aunt Yvonne walked toward the back door, Rosie called to her.

"I thought I told you not to go in the garage," Aunt Yvonne said, her hands on her hips.

"Freddie's hurt. I think he needs stitches in his arm," Rosie said, standing up.

"It hurts! I want my mama! I want Papa!" Freddie began to cry again.

Aunt Yvonne stared at the two of them, her mouth opening

and closing with no words coming out. She bent over, her hands on her thighs, and Rosie could hear her gasping for air.

She ran to her aunt's side. "Are you all right?"

"I can't take it anymore. Not one more thing. It is too much," Aunt Yvonne was saying as she straightened and covered her face with her hands. Her shoulders shook.

"Aunt Yvonne . . ." Rosie began.

"You!" Aunt Yvonne straightened up and turned on Rosie. "You were supposed to watch him. You had your nose stuck in a book again, didn't you?"

Rosie backed away. She had seen Aunt Yvonne mad, but she had never seen the look she was wearing now.

"I don't know what to do with the two of you and I . . . I don't think I can take it any longer." Aunt Yvonne turned away.

Rosie returned to her brother's side. Tears ran silently down his cheeks and she knew he must be in lots of pain. Why couldn't Aunt Yvonne see it as plainly as she could?

"Aloha!" a bright voice sounded from the driveway. "Hello? Is anyone here?"

Rosie turned. It sounded like—but surely it couldn't be . . . ?

Chapter 23

Aunt Etta! Aunt Etta had shown up to rescue them again!

Freddie ran to her. "I don't want to go to the orphanist," he said, still clutching his arm.

"The orphanist? What is he talking about?" she asked Rosie.

"Are my mother and father with you?" Rosie asked, almost afraid to hear the answer.

Aunt Etta shook her head sadly. "Just me, I'm afraid. But we are going to be able—"

"Are you going to take these children?" Aunt Yvonne interrupted. Her face had paled except for two spots of red coloring her cheeks.

"What? Yvonne, what's the matter?" Aunt Etta continued to pat Freddie's back, staggering occasionally as he pressed into her. "Freddie, what's the matter with your arm?" She sank to her knees and tried to examine his injury. Freddie pulled away, clutching the blood-stained towel. "Where did all that blood come from?"

"They are out of control," Aunt Yvonne said. "I don't like to admit it but I cannot handle them."

"He's hurt! How did it happen?" Aunt Etta glared at her sister as she gently unwrapped the towel.

"I don't have any idea. I was doing my part for the war effort and left the two of them here where they obviously were up to no good. At least the little one. She," Aunt Yvonne pointed to Rosie, "probably had her nose in a book while he wreaked havoc."

Freddie sobbed harder. Rosie moved closer to Aunt Etta.

"The important thing now is to take Freddie to a doctor," said Aunt Etta. "He is going to need stitches in this cut."

Rosie handed her a clean towel and Aunt Etta rewrapped Freddie's arm.

"I have no idea who their doctor is!" Aunt Yvonne turned toward the house.

"That's all you have to say? That's it?" Aunt Etta practically spat the words at her sister.

"I will say this." Aunt Yvonne leaned her face close to Aunt Etta's. "Your turn. And after a few days, come back and tell me how you like being saddled with someone else's problems."

"I'm ashamed to call you my sister," Aunt Etta said. "Rosie, pack your and Freddie's things. We need to take care of his arm right away, then we will worry about a place to stay since we will not be staying here." She kissed the top of Freddie's head.

Rosie had never loved her Aunt Etta more. She wished she had the nerve to tell Aunt Yvonne what she thought. She ran into the house and pulled out her few clothes and stuffed them into her schoolbag, then packed Freddie's. She looked around the room for anything she may have forgotten and grabbed the small notebook she had pilfered from one of her aunt's drawers along with the loose pages she had written on. Rosie didn't want to lose another journal!

There was one more thing she wanted to do before she left. Rosie slung a bag over each shoulder and made her way back to the driveway. She dropped them between her aunts, who continued to glare silently at one another.

Rosie slipped into the garage and gathered the presents she was sure belonged to her and Freddie, thanks to her eaves-dropping. E-A-V-E-S-D-R-O-P-P-I-N-G. She checked the tags and, sure enough, the biggest one had Freddie's name on it, from Santa. The two smaller rectangular packages were for her "With love from Mama and Papa."

"What do you think you are doing?" Aunt Yvonne asked when Rosie exited the garage carrying the stack of gifts.

"I don't understand why you didn't give us these gifts on Christmas morning," said Rosie, trying to keep the anger out of her voice. "You must have forgotten where you'd hidden them."

"Those are for . . . those gifts came from . . . there are

children who have much less than the two of you!" Aunt Yvonne finally spit out.

"If they have parents or someone to love them and care for them, someone they can trust to be honest with them, they have all they need," Rosie said.

"Yvonne!" Aunt Etta said and this time her voice was full of disappointment.

"Etta, it is not your place to speak to me in that tone of voice. You know that being the youngest, you never have to take on any of the nasty tasks—"

Aunt Etta interrupted, "In case you've already forgotten, I was released, today, from an internment camp where I was being detained just because my last name is Rauschling, which is also your last name."

"My name is Bell," Aunt Yvonne corrected her. She walked quickly into the house, shutting the door firmly behind her.

Aunt Etta shook her head. "Don't take her words to heart," she said. "Something must have happened today. It's never taken much to put Yvonne into a spin. I'm sure she and Uncle Charles love you just as I do."

"No, they don't," Rosie said. Freddie nodded in agreement. "They may feel responsible for us, but Aunt Yvonne doesn't love us like you do, uh-uh, not at all. She makes us be quiet all the time, and she doesn't want anybody to know we are her family. She tells people we are refugees."

Aunt Etta's eyes filled with tears. "Oh, my darlings! I am so sorry." She tried to pull both of them into a hug, but Freddie pulled away. "I love you. And your mother and father love you and they miss you very, very much. And we are going straight to a doctor to have you sewn up before more of your stuffing falls out!"

"Where are they? Mama and Papa?" Rosie asked. She basked in the feel of Aunt Etta's arms around her. It was like the sun finally came out after a long, cold rain. "Are they— were you—at Fort Armstrong? I went to visit. The soldiers wouldn't let me in."

"When was that?" Aunt Etta asked, her forehead wrinkled in puzzlement. "I have been there every minute from the time I was arrested until today when they let me out on parole."

"Parole?" Rosie said. P-A-R-O-L-E.

"I have to report in every month, but that doesn't matter. I am here now, with you."

"Where are we going to live now?" Freddie asked.

"Your parents have a house they usually rent out, here in Honolulu, on the Diamond Head side of the island," Aunt Etta said.

"I know that house!" said Rosie. "I sort of remember living there, before Mama opened the kindergarten and we moved to the valley."

"That's right. And we are going there. We will have to find Mr. Smith, the man handling your parents' properties first—or second, after we visit the doctor."

And there was that name again. "And Mama and Papa? You haven't told us where they are yet," said Rosie.

"They are moving your mother from Fort Armstrong and your papa, he is I'm not sure where. The men were sent to the mainland . . ."

"We'll never see Papa again if he is on the mainland!"

Freddie started to sob again, louder.

"Your mama and I were in the women's section, apart from your papa, but at least the two of us were together. Now they are moving all the people they call 'enemy aliens,' Germans, Japanese, Italians alike, to Sand Island. I think you will be able to visit your mama there. And your papa, when he returns."

Aunt Etta sounded so certain of everything when Rosie wasn't certain about anything.

"Why do they call you enemies? And aliens? You were born here!" Rosie said.

"I wish I knew." Aunt Etta sighed.

The three of them stood in silence on Aunt Yvonne's driveway. Rosie did not want to let Aunt Etta out of her sight, ever again. Having her young aunt beside her made everything better.

"Fortunately, I have George's car for the afternoon. He is lucky to have a gas ration and a car still because of his job with the news service. Now, don't forget your gas masks and your ID cards," Aunt Etta reminded.

Rosie made a face but gathered the masks from their place beside the back door. She knew she should be glad she'd never had to use the mask, but they were a pain to carry everywhere just in case.

When they returned, Aunt Etta looked at the two bags at her feet. "That's it? That's all you brought?" she asked.

Rosie nodded as she flung both her and Freddie's gas mask over her shoulder. "And no one knows where the rest of our things are. Even Kitty is gone." Rosie halted on the walk to the car for a moment, missing her pet.

"Oh, darling! Is there nothing sacred in these different days?" Aunt Etta murmured, more to herself than to Rosie.

Chapter 24

Freddie needed six stitches in the cut on his arm. The nurse told him he had been as brave as any soldier she had worked on as she taped a bandage over the cut. Freddie beamed at the praise.

Once they had finished at the doctor's, Aunt Etta leaned against the car seat and closed her eyes for a moment. "I think it's still early enough to go find this Mr. Smith," she said.

"Me, too!" Rosie agreed. She wanted very much to meet this mysterious Mr. Smith she'd only heard about and seen from a hiding place on the stairs.

"When can we open the presents?" Freddie asked, holding the one marked to him across his lap.

"You must feel better," said Aunt Etta.

"You can tell everyone you have a war wound," Rosie said.

Freddie grinned. "And the nurse said I was brave as a soldier."

"You do and you were," Aunt Etta said, "but let's save the present for when we land someplace for the night."

It meant another Christmas celebration, this time with Aunt Etta. Rosie could wait. She patted the presents on the car seat beside her and wished she had something for Aunt Etta even though no present could ever show how glad they were to have her back.

Aunt Etta drove slowly and carefully through heavy traffic, asking Rosie to keep an eye out for the address Mama had given her for Mr. Smith's office. "How can there be so many cars when gas is rationed and cars are supposed to be only for certain purposes?" Aunt Etta said.

Rosie didn't realize gas was rationed. Aunt Yvonne had said there were food shortages because things were slow to arrive from the mainland and that was why they ate what she called "light meals."

"They're from the Army," said Freddie. Rosie watched him try to take it all in, turning his head from side to side and leaning out the open car window. "So many soldiers!" he said.

"So many sandbags," Rosie said.

Finally, Aunt Etta found a parking spot near where Mr. Smith's office was supposed to be and they piled out of the car. "We could have taken a minute to freshen up," she said, smoothing Rosie's hair and straightening her dress. "I hope we can get the bloodstains out." She touched where Freddie had bled on Rosie. "What will Mr. Smith think I have been doing with the two of you!"

Freddie pulled away as Aunt Etta tried to comb his hair with her fingers. It ended up standing on end making him look like some kind of rooster. "You need a haircut in the worst way!" she said to him.

"I want all my hair cut off, like a soldier's," he said.

"We'll see," said Aunt Etta. "For now, please wipe your mouth and your nose." She handed him a handkerchief from her purse. She also pulled out a compact and checked her hair, then freshened her lipstick.

Rosie hung on one of Aunt Etta's arms and Freddie hung on the other as if they were afraid she would disappear if they let go.

The sign on the office at the address said simply ISLAND REALTY. Aunt Etta held the door open for Rosie and Freddie to go in before her.

Inside, Aunt Etta walked up to the desk where Mr. Smith sat. He smiled broadly when he looked at her, but the smile dimmed when he noticed Rosie and Freddie standing behind her. Freddie held on to his aunt's skirt, but Rosie stood as tall as she could and faced the man directly. He was definitely the man who had brought the presents to Aunt Yvonne's house.

"What can I do for you today, miss?" Mr. Smith asked, pleasantly enough.

"I'm Marietta Rauschling, sister of Greta Schatzer," Aunt

Etta introduced herself. "Greta informed me you are taking care of their properties?"

"So many properties! All of these people who are being detained . . ."

"I'm sure you are very busy, but we need to know only about the Schatzer properties," Aunt Etta said.

"Schatzer, Schatzer." Mr. Smith looked puzzled as he shuffled papers on his desk.

Rosie stepped forward, gathering courage from Aunt Etta beside her. "Maybe I can help you remember. One of the properties, the one in the valley, you sold to Malia Kamaka."

"What?" Aunt Etta said. "You didn't say anything about this. How do you know?" she asked Rosie before she turned to Mr. Smith for his answer.

Mr. Smith's face reddened. "I have had to sell so many properties." He rummaged through more papers.

"Rosie?" Aunt Etta said.

"Rainer took me to the house and Malia was there. She said she'd bought it from a Mr. Smith and was going to live there and open a nursery school," Rosie said, looking at Aunt Etta, then Mr. Smith, then back to her aunt.

"Ah, yes, the property with the nursery school on the ground floor." Mr. Smith shook his head. "I'm afraid I had to sell that one to meet expenses that seem to mount up faster than you can keep track." He pulled out a folder and opened it.

"You sold it! Do my sister and brother-in-law know about

this?" Aunt Etta leaned on the desk, almost touching Mr. Smith's nose with her own.

"I have complete authority to do what is necessary. Your sister and her husband signed papers giving me that right." Mr. Smith scooted his chair back and waved papers at Aunt Etta.

"That is simply unbelievable," Aunt Etta said.

"What about our furniture? Our clothes? Where are they?" Rosie asked, taking heart from her aunt.

"In storage. Quite impossible to access at this point," said Mr. Smith, "and one of the reasons for the mounting expenses."

Rosie swallowed hard. "The cat?" she asked in little more than a whisper.

"Cat? I wouldn't know about that. Never saw a cat," he said sharply. "Cats can take care of themselves, little girl. I wouldn't worry about it."

Rosie stared at the floor. Kitty had never learned to take care of herself because she'd always been cared for. Kitty had been her princess like she had been her papa's. Both of them had to care for themselves in these different days. Aunt Etta stroked Rosie's hair, but it only reminded her of how she did the same with Kitty. She pulled away.

"I am sure this isn't the last you will hear about the selling of the valley property," Aunt Etta said, "but for now Greta and Henry would like you to make the Honolulu house available for us to live in. I will be taking care of their children until . . ." she shrugged, "for the foreseeable future."

Now Mr. Smith's expression changed again, becoming very sad. *He should be an actor*, Rosie thought.

Freddie had wandered away and stood before a pile of furniture and assorted knick-knacks piled at the back of Mr. Smith's office. "Hey!" he said, pulling a lamp out of the pile. "We have one like this." He turned it round and round.

Rosie looked over Mr. Smith's shoulder and recognized the lamp as exactly like the one that used to sit on Mama's desk. It had the same green shade and yellow pineapple-shaped base. Rosie walked toward the pile, wanting to see more. There was, she noticed from a distance, a stack of quilts on the bottom shelf that looked interesting. Some of the color patterns were familiar, matching ones that were missing from their house.

"Hey!" Mr. Smith's face had turned a deep red and he was no longer trying to sound nice. "Get away from there. Those belong to the families I'm watching out for." He started to rise from his chair.

"Rosie! Freddie! Come back here and leave Mr. Smith's things alone."

Reluctantly, Rosie backed away, pulling Freddie with her.

"The house you were speaking of," Mr. Smith said, shaking his head. "I am so sorry but the government has taken a lease on that house. So many men coming to the island because of the war and so little housing available for them. I had to remove the family living there because who says no to the government? I have mixed feelings when I tell you all your sister's property is occupied at present."

"So, we have no place to live?" Aunt Etta said as if she didn't believe it.

"Hmm." Mr. Smith pulled some papers toward him. "I do have one property, small, very small, one bedroom, a living room/kitchen, but it is close to the beach and it is open. I could lease that one to you." He pushed a paper across the desk to Aunt Etta.

She read it over, then gasped. "That can't be the rental price!"

"I am afraid it is. Like I said, there's great demand for property right now."

"Then may I ask you what kind of allowance we will be receiving from the properties you are managing for Henry and Greta?"

"Allowance?" Mr. Smith laughed. "It is taking every penny and more to take care of these places. I've had to make repairs, pay taxes, insurance. I am so very sorry, my dear, but there will be no allowance. Now, do you want the house or not? I will not require a deposit, how about that? I can tell from the look on your face that you are disappointed in our meeting. You should have called and I could have saved you a trip."

Rosie's stomach started aching. What did it mean that there was no house and no allowance? Would they have to go back to live with Aunt Yvonne?

"I would like to look at the house," Aunt Etta said.

"Normally, I would go along, but I have an appointment soon." Mr. Smith looked at his watch, then leaned across his desk and pulled a set of keys off a board hanging to the side. "Here you go."

Aunt Etta grabbed the keys. "Th—" came out of her mouth, then she shook her head as she cut off the word midway, grabbed Freddie by the wrist, motioned for Rosie to follow her, and walked out of the office.

Chapter 25

No one said a word on the way to the car. Rosie climbed into the front passenger seat, Freddie into the back. Aunt Etta opened the car door but paused before climbing inside. When she finally did, she slammed the door and hit the steering wheel once, then again and again.

"Do we have to live with Aunt Yvonne after all?" Rosie asked softly.

"You do not. We will find a way to make this work." Aunt Etta backed quickly out of the parking spot and sped toward the beach. They drove through an area of elegant hotels and saw Diamond Head glistening in the distance like the jewel it was named for. Neighborhoods appeared with the houses growing smaller and more worn as they found the area where the rental house was located. Finally, Aunt Etta stopped the car and they stared at the tiny house sitting back from the road.

"It's a dump," Aunt Etta said.

Rosie leaned around her aunt for a better look. The front of the house had one window and a door painted bright blue. Several white shingles were missing from the sides and front and the yard was mostly dirt. There was, however, a magnificently tall coconut tree in the yard with lovely fresh coconuts hanging off it. And Rosie could smell the ocean and feel a slight breeze through the car window.

When she looked toward the beach, a mix of feelings came over her. The water was clear and blue as always with sunlight dancing across the waves, but barbed wire lined the sand blocking their way. The sight of that barbed wire was scary. Rosie knew it was there to make it harder for anyone to get onto the island—not just anyone, but the Japs, she supposed.

"According to the paper that man gave me, it is furnished as well," Aunt Etta continued.

"Let's go look," Rosie said. She didn't care what kind of house they had to live in if it meant they would be together and away from Aunt Yvonne.

"I'll have to find a job," Aunt Etta went on. "Are you all right with watching Freddie while I work?"

"Sure. I've been watching him anyway and all Aunt Yvonne did was sit around and read magazines or go out for her 'war work.'"

"If I believed that horrid man, that he was truly spending your parents' money to take care of their property, I'd feel better about this."

"He stole our lamp," said Freddie, leaning over the seat.

"It was a lamp that looked like yours, dear," Aunt Etta corrected him. "There are dozens, no probably hundreds, of those pineapple lamps in Hawaii."

"It was ours. There was a chip out of one of the pineapple leaves and I was the one who threw the ball that took the chip out," said Freddie.

"He did!" Rosie agreed. "Ours was chipped. And I saw a stack of quilts that could have been Mama's. I told myself they weren't, but they could be. I wish I could have seen them closer."

Aunt Etta sighed. "I don't know what to say to that."

"Call the police! Report Mr. Smith?" said Rosie.

"For a chipped lamp? And don't forget, I am . . . I just . . . well, I can't." Aunt Etta stared at her hands in her lap. Her nail polish was chipped and her nails chewed.

Aunt Etta couldn't call the police because she was German and on parole, Rosie realized. She reached over and squeezed her aunt's hand. It was a fact they had to live with. "Thank you for all you are doing for us."

Aunt Etta's eyes sparkled with tears. She leaned over and kissed Rosie's cheek. "I can't even keep my job as a freelance photographer, though there's more work than ever. They confiscated my camera. I might be taking pictures and giving them to the Nazis to let them know all our island secrets. At least that's what I think the government is afraid of. No one will tell us anything about why we were arrested."

C-O-N-F-I-S-C-A-T-E-D. Rosie's breath caught. She remembered the government man who had asked her about the photos that had been hanging in the hallway, how she'd proudly said her aunt had taken them. Was that why Aunt Etta had been interned? Was it her fault? Rosie didn't have the heart to ask. Not yet.

"Shall we take a look at our new abode?" Aunt Etta asked.

"Abode? What's that?" Freddie asked.

"Our house, my dear, our home," she said softly.

Freddie ran toward the door. "I win!" he said. "That means I can choose my room first."

Aunt Etta unlocked the front door and Freddie entered.

Rosie examined the house from the doorway. She could see almost all of it. The front room had a sagging orange couch and a matching chair. There was no rug on the scratched wood floor. It was open to the kitchen where there was a small cooking stove and what might be an icebox. There were two cabinets and a sink with a water pump. A table with three rickety chairs took up most of the kitchen floor, which was covered with a stained and peeling grayish linoleum.

Rosie walked through the living room and found the bedroom that looked almost like it had been attached as an afterthought. One bed took up most of the space. The bathroom that was tucked into the corner of the room with only a toilet and sink was definitely added on. The only privacy was behind a plastic curtain, no door at all.

"Maybe Yvonne will lend us some linens and towels,"

Aunt Etta said as she opened the cabinets. "There are dishes here."

Rosie checked the dishes, a mishmash of color and patterns. Most of them were chipped or cracked, but again, she didn't care as long as she was with Aunt Etta.

"We don't need towels," said Freddie. "There's no bathtub."

Aunt Etta checked the bedroom. "Great," she said, "that is just great."

"It is!" Freddie insisted with a grin. "It's like a playhouse. I like it!"

Rosie had to smile at her brother. He was making lemonade out of their lemons.

"And now can we open the presents?" Freddie asked.

"Of course. I wish we had Christmas cake or something to celebrate with," Aunt Etta said.

Freddie had already disappeared outside. He reappeared minutes later with the three gifts and . . . a coconut. "This was on the ground, but it looks good. We can crack it open and drink the milk and eat the coconut."

"You are such a smart boy!" said Aunt Etta as she carried the coconut to the kitchen.

Freddie tossed Rosie's presents to her and immediately ripped the paper off the big box with his name on it. "Soldiers! I got soldiers!" he shouted so loudly that Rosie was sure her mama at Fort Armstrong must be able to hear how happy he was.

Rosie opened her first gift, a copy of *Little Women*, exactly what she had asked for. She stroked the cover with its picture of the four little women gathered around their mother. How cozy the room in the picture looked with its big chair and fireplace. She set it aside and opened the second package—a new journal with a new pen. Rosie wished she could tell Mama and Papa thank you. They'd managed to find exactly what she wanted.

Rosie opened the journal, and immediately started writing.

We have a new home. With Aunt Etta. And a coconut tree. We visited Mr. Smith, the man caring for Mama and Papa's properties, but I am suspicious of him. He said we can't live in any of the houses. And he had what Freddie and I both think is our pineapple lamp, although he said it wasn't. I plan to keep an eye on this Mr. Smith.

I also thought of someone who might have "informed" on Mama. Chester's mom. For some reason I remembered Chester – I know he's just a baby – said his mother thought our mama might be a Nazi. If she truly thought that, she might have acted on it. And Malia seemed to have thoughts about Mama and Papa being Nazis as well. But she wouldn't, would she? Even if she has taken over our house.

Rosie had known Malia for so long, it was hard to think she might do something so awful. But she reluctantly added Malia to her suspect list.

Chapter 26

The new house turned out to be not that bad. Rosie was surprised to find out that with her tanned skin, dark hair, and faded dresses, she was accepted as part Hawaiian, part *haole* by the other kids in the neighborhood with no question and no questions about where her mother and father were. Everyone figured Aunt Etta was their mother, never mind she was closer in age to being a big sister. Still, the acceptance came as a huge relief to Rosie after Aunt Yvonne, Rainer, and what she imagined as the whole population of Honolulu had made her feel ashamed of her German heritage and required to hide who she was and where her parents were.

George thought he could find Aunt Etta a job at his newspaper but as soon as the editor found out she was an "enemy alien parolee," he told George she was a security risk and they couldn't hire her after all.

Rosie watched Freddie, who spent most of his time playing with his soldiers or on the beach with a gang of new friends, while Aunt Etta looked for work. Rosie, when she wasn't hanging out with neighborhood kids jumping rope, playing hopscotch, or talking about movies and movie stars, spent her days writing in her journal, reading, and working on the quilt square Kealani had given her. And she finally had enough to read! One of her new friends, Betty, had told them there was a public library nearby, and Aunt Etta had taken Rosie and Freddie to sign up for library cards. Rosie didn't feel as lonely when she had books to keep her company.

As she waited for Aunt Etta to come home, Rosie wrote in her journal:

We now have come to a truce with Aunt Yvonne. She brought us towels and some food (including Spam) for the house. Aunt Etta said Aunt Yvonne is "nervous" people will find out about her German heritage and that's why she didn't want to keep us. That it wasn't because she didn't love us. I am still not sure.

I am trying to figure out a plan to find out where our property, clothes and stuff, is. I think I need to put Mr. Smith under surveillance.

Before she could finish writing out her plan, Aunt Etta breezed in from job hunting.

"Success!" she announced, her arms full of bags with the smell of food wafting from them, a smell that made Rosie's mouth water. "I have a job." Aunt Etta placed the bags on the kitchen table and hugged Rosie.

Rosie was glad for her aunt and for them—but she mostly wanted to know what smelled so good. "At a restaurant?" she asked, realizing they would never have the money to buy two bags of food!

"A food stand," Aunt Etta said, "on the beach. And I can bring home leftovers, when there are leftovers. Plus, my boss let me have extra tonight so I could 'get to know the menu.' I think he realized I had no money for food. But I don't care why he gave us food. It's a feast!"

Freddie burst into the house at that moment and grabbed Aunt Etta and held her tight around the waist. Every day it was the same. When she arrived home, Freddie couldn't get enough of her, touching her, talking to her, staying tight by her side as if she might disappear any minute. Rosie knew exactly how he felt.

"C'mon, let's eat!" Aunt Etta pulled sandwiches and hamburgers and even two pieces of pie out of the paper bags. "And then I'll change that bandage on your arm. How's it doing?"

"I just tell everybody I got wounded in the war. It doesn't even hurt anymore," said Freddie. He pulled out his chair and sat down.

Before moving to the beach, Rosie never remembered being hungry, truly and really hungry. But in the week since they'd moved from Aunt Yvonne's, it sometimes felt like her entire body was empty.

Aunt Etta had tried her best, but the money only went so far. Aunt Yvonne, Rosie knew, had given Aunt Etta a little money, probably to make sure they didn't show up back at the house. But Rosie had also spent a lot of time climbing the coconut tree outside their front door and throwing down the nuts to Freddie. After the war, she vowed, she would never eat another coconut ever. Aunt Etta had also shown them which kinds of seaweeds were edible and they sometimes ate that—mixed with coconut.

Every time her stomach growled, Rosie found she could not help thinking about Mr. Smith refusing to give them money and the pineapple lamp that Freddie insisted was from their house. She knew if Nancy Drew was there, she would figure out a way to prove Mr. Smith had taken their belongings. But perhaps she could, too. Once her stomach was full, she would make a plan.

"Freddie," Rosie said as soon as Aunt Etta had left for work the next day, "let's take a walk. Okay?"

"I was going to play battle with some of the guys," Freddie complained. "And this time I can be a pilot. I decided I want to be a pilot and not a gun soldier. What do you think?"

"I hope you never have to be either one," said Rosie. She knew from reading the papers George left behind when he had time to visit that there were soldiers—and pilots—being killed every day. Freddie still looked at war as a game.

"I can't go and leave you here and I want to check out Mr. Smith and all that stuff he had," she said, sharing her plan with her brother.

"Freddie," Rosie said, "it will be like we are detectives

investigating." I-N-V-E-S-T-I-G-A-T-I-N-G, she spelled to herself as she struggled to convince her brother to come along with her. "We can call it The Mystery of Our Disappearing Belongings."

"I can be a detective, too? With you?" Freddie looked like he didn't quite trust her to let him help.

"I need you," she said.

"I guess," Freddie finally agreed. "I wish we had magnifying glasses and badges and . . ."

"We're more the kind of detective that figures stuff out with our brains," Rosie said. She wished Leilani were here to be a detective with her instead of her younger brother. Even Betty, who liked to read, didn't have the same interest in mysteries as she did.

Rosie and Freddie scuffed along in the sand at the side of the road until they got close enough to town for there to be sidewalks. Neither wore shoes. Rosie had outgrown hers and Freddie didn't bother with the sandals he'd gotten from the Palus.

Once in the downtown area, everywhere Rosie looked there were soldiers. None of them carried guns around town but the sheer number of them was scary enough. Up ahead she noticed a knot of soldiers, standing in front of a brightly painted building, talking and smoking. She pulled Freddie into the road to walk around them. As soon as they passed by, several of the boys broke out in laughter. Rosie felt her face heat up and pulled at her dress to make sure it was down as far as it would go. It was starting to feel short at the bottom and tight around the top. If only she'd quit growing until they could afford at least one new dress that fit.

Rosie spotted Mr. Smith's office sign hanging over the sidewalk a block ahead. Parked in front was a big shiny Packard like Uncle Charles's that had to cost a lot of money. This car was much nicer than the one he'd driven to Aunt Yvonne's only a week ago. And the parking spot said RESERVED FOR LAWRENCE L. SMITH. Where did he find the money to buy an expensive car?

When they reached a spot where she could see Mr. Smith's office but he couldn't see them, Rosie halted. "We are going to wait here and see what Mr. Smith is up to," she whispered to Freddie.

"Here? In the hot sun?" Freddie leaned against the building, kicking his foot against the wall.

"We have him under surveillance," Rosie said. S-U-R-V-E-I-L-L-A-N-C-E, she spelled nervously to herself. Why couldn't she give up the spelling practice? There wouldn't be a spelling championship after all this time and even if there was, she wouldn't be at the same school to participate.

"Let's go," Freddie whined after only a few minutes.

Rosie shushed him and watched the office.

Before Freddie could complain again, Mr. Smith appeared, looked right then left and locked his office door. He carried a wooden box under his arm.

Rosie held Freddie back as he tried to rush forward. She waited to see if the man would drive or walk away.

She felt lucky for once when he passed his car and continued to walk down the sidewalk.

Rosie motioned for her brother to stay behind her but to follow.

"Where are we going?" he asked in a loud whisper.

"Let's see where *he* goes," she answered in a much quieter whisper.

The breath of Freddie's sigh was strong enough to ruffle her hair.

Only a few blocks farther down the street, Mr. Smith turned into a small shop.

Rosie glanced in the big picture window as they walked slowly past and saw him place the box on the counter. He opened it and the man behind the counter pawed through the contents. She picked up speed and at the corner crossed the street, pulling Freddie by the wrist as he poked along.

She walked back in the direction they had come, slowly, waiting to see if Mr. Smith came out. The window had the name JEWELS OF THE SEA written across it in fancy script. Rosie figured, given the name, it must be a jewelry store.

"You said we wouldn't be long," Freddie whined.

"Just a few more minutes. Let's see what he's doing in there," Rosie answered.

"That wasn't our box," Freddie said.

"No, but it was someone's box. Shh!" Mr. Smith stepped out of the shop, without the box, and Rosie glimpsed a flash of green as his hand disappeared inside his pocket. Money?

"Can we go now?" Freddie asked.

Rosie stayed across the street, tracking Mr. Smith as he retraced his steps, soon unlocking and turning into his office.

Hmm, her new journal would be a perfect place to record every suspicious action Mr. Smith committed. She should have brought it along.

"Now? Can we go now?" Freddie whined.

Rosie nodded and let her brother lead the way.

As Rosie and Freddie passed by an alley where a row of Hawaiian women sat weaving nets, Rosie heard the strains of ukulele music. When she glanced in the direction of the music, she was so surprised at who she saw playing that she stopped abruptly. Freddie backtracked to join her.

"Hey, it's Rosie!" a boy's voice called out. The music stopped.

"Hi, Kam," Rosie answered, pleased that he remembered her. It had been a couple of weeks since he'd shown her to the bomb shelter.

Kam laid down his yellow ukulele and joined Rosie and Freddie at the entrance to the alley.

"I thought maybe you'd joined your parents," Kam said.

Rosie shook her head and felt her face heat. The way Kam said it was as if it was normal to have parents interned, but she still didn't like the reminder that they had been locked away. "We moved to the beach," she added and described the neighborhood where they'd ended up.

"I know that place. I live pretty close. Do you surf?" he asked.

"I want to learn," Freddie interrupted. "We were learning and then . . ." He stopped, looking at Rosie.

"Our neighbors joined the Army," she finished for him.

"I can teach you." Kam rubbed Freddie's head. Freddie had talked Aunt Etta into letting him cut his hair close to his head, like a soldier, and he was very proud of his hairstyle.

"When?" Freddie asked. "Except I don't have a surfboard."

"I have one. Hmm, I can come by," he looked at Rosie, "not sure when, but soon." He shrugged. "I need to help out the aunties part of most days, but if it's all right with you . . ."

Rosie nodded. "Should be around. With no school . . ."

"I heard it won't be long before it starts. But if you stay where you're living now, we should be assigned the same school. What brings you down here?"

"We're detectives and we are investigating Mr. Smith," Freddie said.

Rosie felt her face heat up. That must sound so childish to Kam.

"He has some of our stuff and we want it back," Freddie continued as Rosie gave him a warning look.

"You mean that guy in the office across the street?" Kam asked. "Strange things going on over there. And he was there when they took all the radios from your father's shop."

"He was? I guess it could be because he is the one supposedly taking care of our properties," Rosie said, but she didn't entirely believe that he had her parents' or anyone's but his own best interests in mind. Not when she'd witnessed him selling a box of jewelry.

"What do you mean about strange things going on at his office?" Rosie asked.

"I don't know. I've seen trucks pull up and unload stuff, house stuff. What does someone who *sells* houses need with lamps and chairs and dishes? Or radios for that matter. And that's his business, or it was before the war. I think now he does stuff for the government, with enemy aliens." Kam stopped short. "At least that's what I heard my auntie say."

"Today, we saw him take a box to a jewelry store and when he came out," Rosie paused, "he didn't have it any longer but he was putting something, money I think, in his pocket. Like he's selling things. I don't think that is what my parents had in mind when they asked him to take care of their property." What valuables of theirs were worth selling? Their pineapple lamp wasn't worth anything. But her mother's jewelry and the quilts were also gone. Everything was gone! In storage, Mr. Smith said. He could be telling the truth, but she didn't trust him. He had sold their home to Malia! Why wouldn't he sell more of their things?

"I can play the ukulele," Freddie said, looking at the instrument Kam had left in the alleyway.

"You're a regular Hawaiian beach boy," Kam said.

"No, I want to be a soldier," said Freddie seriously.

"So Rosie," Kam poked her in the arm, pulling her out of her thoughts, "okay if I come by sometime?"

"Sure, I guess so," she said with a shrug. "See you then."

"Bring your surfboard," Freddie called to Kam as Rosie turned Freddie toward home.

Chapter 27

Freddie refused to go spy on Mr. Smith during the next week, so Rosie couldn't, either. Rosie hoped that he wasn't selling something that belonged to them when she wasn't watching. She'd convinced herself that it was the quilts that he would have the best chance of selling and making money. Two days into 1942 and she had nothing to write in her journal.

Rosie made it a point to work every day on the quilt square Kealani had given her. She kept reminding herself that Kealani had said her parents would return when she finished it *if* there was enough aloha spirit sewn into the design. Rosie tried to think only positive thoughts when she was quilting.

Rosie was concentrating on making her stitches even tinier when Freddie slammed into the house.

"I don't have anything to do." Freddie threw himself on the couch and it gave out a scary groan like it might collapse.

"Where are all your little soldier friends?" Rosie asked, wondering if the piece of furniture would last out their stay.

"We aren't little," said Freddie. "They're busy or have to go someplace with their mothers." His lower lip trembled.

Rosie set her quilt square aside. "Let's walk downtown . . ."

"And spy some more?"

"We can walk by Mr. Smith's office on our way," Rosie said.

"On our way where?"

"I don't know. Maybe we'll have an adventure." Rosie stood up and grabbed the key Aunt Etta had left for them. "Maybe we'll see Kam."

"I don't have anything else to do so I guess I'll go," Freddie said, but stayed on the couch.

"When?" Rosie asked, tapping her toe.

"Okay, okay. I don't know what your hurry is."

Rosie locked the door and hung the key around her neck, tucking it inside her dress. She took off and Freddie walked behind, dragging a stick through the dirt.

As they walked deeper into the busy shopping district, Rosie felt like she was seeing the same group of soldiers she'd seen the last time they walked down the main street. She turned toward Mr. Smith's office.

Kam was leaning against the wall outside the alley. He waved them over. "I was hoping to see you. Sorry I haven't been out to your house yet but I've been busy delivering nets for the aunties. They've really stepped it up. Soon all the buildings in Honolulu will be covered," he said.

"Has anything been happening there?" Rosie asked, pointing at Mr. Smith's office. And then, as if she could make him appear by wishing, Mr. Smith walked out of his doorway, carrying quilts piled in his arms. "Quilts!" she said in a squeaky voice.

"Our mama had quilts," Freddie informed him. "But now they're gone, Rosie said."

Rosie felt like she might finally find out something if—and it was a big if—any one of those quilts was her mother's.

"Are they Mama's?" Freddie whispered.

"Shh!" Rosie placed her finger over her lips.

"There are lots of Hawaiian quilts on this island," Kam said, seeming to dismiss what Rosie considered important. She ignored him, not taking her eyes off Mr. Smith.

He struggled to keep the pile of quilts from shifting as he walked.

Rosie gave Mr. Smith a head start, then followed. The boys trailed behind her.

Mr. Smith turned a corner. Rosie motioned for the boys to wait, then they ran to catch up.

They walked farther away from the busiest part of town before the man paused before a wooden door. He leaned back as if to read the name on the window, tucked the quilts under one arm and pushed the door open.

Again, Rosie motioned for the boys to stay where they were as she crossed the street to try to read the sign on the window.

Crisscrossed tape made the words almost illegible. I-L-L-E-G-I-B-L-E. But the shop sign said exactly what she'd expected: Quilts of Hawaii. Still, she cautioned herself not to jump to conclusions. He could be asking the owner to store them or display them. Or, as she suspected most likely, to buy them.

Rosie moved to the side of the window, trying to stay unseen yet able to see Mr. Smith. The boys crossed the street and joined her.

"I'm thirsty," Freddie whispered.

"Later. You know we can't afford to buy anything."

"But it's so hot," he complained.

"Shh!"

"When we go back, Auntie has some drinks she'll let us have," Kam said.

"Where did he go?" Freddie asked.

"In there," Rosie pointed.

Freddie dropped to his knees and peeked up through the front window. "He's showing some quilts to the shopkeeper. They are spread out all over the counter."

"Has she given him any money?" Rosie asked.

"Nope, she's pointing at quilts all around the room. There are a lot of quilts in there!" Freddie said. "And now Mr. Smith is folding one of the quilts up, but no! She's grabbing it and looking at it again."

Rosie couldn't stand not knowing what was happening. She placed her hands around her eyes to shade the sun and looked through the window. The shopkeeper immediately looked up at her and waved at her to go away. Before Mr. Smith could turn around, Rosie pulled back.

"Did any of them look like Mama's quilts?" she asked Freddie.

"I don't know! I don't remember!"

It was killing Rosie to have to wait to see if any of the quilts the man had belonged to her family. "We'll have to wait for him to come out and I'll go in and see if they are Mama's," she said. "We'd better wait over there." They moved to a shadier spot.

When Mr. Smith finally came out of the shop, without the quilts, he paused on the sidewalk, took out a handkerchief and wiped his face. He seemed to look right at Rosie and the boys, but then right past them.

Mr. Smith stuck his handkerchief in his suit coat pocket and headed back the way he had come. When he was far enough away that Rosie was sure he was on his way back to his office, she motioned for Freddie and Kam to follow her back to the quilt shop.

Rosie opened the door to the quilt shop slowly while Freddie hung back. Kam stayed with him. "You don't need us," Kam said. "I have a feeling if too many kids come in the shop, it will make that lady nervous. She didn't even like you looking in the window!"

"Then wait over there in the shade. I won't be long." Rosie stepped inside.

"What you want, girlie?" the Hawaiian shopkeeper asked. There was a pile of quilts on the counter in front of her.

"My, um, my mother really loves quilts and it is her birthday soon," Rosie said. "I, I mean we were thinking maybe we could buy her one for her bedroom."

The woman laughed loud and heartily. "You want to buy one of my quilts?"

"Did you make all of these?" Rosie asked.

Again the woman laughed. "No, no, they come from all the islands. Authentic Hawaiian quilts." She ran her hand over the top of one of the quilts in front of her.

"You should learn to quilt and make one for your mama, I think," the woman said as she looked Rosie up and down. "You cannot afford my authentic Hawaiian quilts."

Rosie felt her entire body heat up. She knew her hair was messy and her dress tight and worn, but this woman knew nothing about her. She continued toward the counter. She wanted to take a closer look at the quilts on the counter. Quickly she turned up the corner of the pink and white quilt on top and saw the familiar initials of Auntie Palu. The quilt underneath Auntie Palu's sported a set of initials belonging to neither her mama nor Auntie.

The woman quickly smacked Rosie's hand away. She didn't hit hard, but Rosie wasn't used to being struck for any reason. She pulled her hand back and cradled it against her chest. Feeling the burn of tears, she turned.

The door opened and Rosie stopped in her tracks. "Auntie Palu!" she said. "What are you doing here?"

"I could ask you the same question," said Auntie Palu, drawing Rosie into a hug.

Leilani followed her mother into the shop.

"Hi," Rosie greeted her.

"Hi," Leilani said quietly. She shifted her weight from side to side.

Rosie wished she was wearing one of the nicer dresses Leilani had passed along to her, but she'd been saving them for school. "Thank you so much for the clothes. They will make all the difference when school starts."

Auntie Palu had moved to the counter and spoke in a low voice to the clerk.

"I know those were some of the clothes you liked, and they probably look better on you than on me anyway," Leilani said with a shrug.

Rosie couldn't hold back any longer. "I miss you so much!" she burst out.

"Me, too." Leilani reached up and wiped away a tear. "I am sorry I was such a . . ." she looked over her shoulder at her mother then whispered, "loser. Everything was starting to change. I was so upset you might go to a new school. And then there was the spelling bee. I know you are a better speller than I am. And I wanted to win so bad."

"And neither of those things matter. I'll go to a different school no matter what now that Malia lives in our house, and I won't be in the spelling bee if I'm at a different school."

"If they even have a spelling bee!" Leilani said. "I've been so busy helping Mama entertain soldiers that I haven't had a chance to even look at the words. And I'm sorry I . . ." she paused, "borrowed your list."

"Like you said, I wasn't using it," said Rosie. "And you did me a favor. You saved it from being taken with the rest of our stuff."

"I am glad to see my girls together again," said Auntie Palu.

"Auntie, look at those quilts on the counter," Rosie said, turning her attention back to what had brought her into the shop in the first place.

"Ahh! Looks like very good," Auntie Palu murmured as she surveyed the pile, then pulled her quilt out of the pile. "This one I made for my good friends the Schatzers! Where you get it?"

"That is my quilt now," the shop owner said, taking hold of it. "I paid good money for it."

That was exactly what Rosie was waiting to hear. She had been right. Mr. Smith was selling things he'd taken from their house.

"But it is stolen, taken without permission," said Auntie Palu.

"The man said he was selling it for some . . ." the shop owner lowered her voice, "*internees*. That he was taking care of their property and they needed the money."

All true, thought Rosie, *except the internees never see the money.*

"I will give you the money you paid for the quilt. How much?" Auntie Palu asked.

"No, Auntie Palu, you can't do that!" Rosie said, taking Auntie's arm and trying to pull her away from the counter.

The shop keeper named a price.

"That is all!" Auntie Palu exclaimed. "My quilt is worth more than that!" She threw some money on the counter, gathered the quilt, and motioned for the girls to follow her from the shop.

"Auntie, you are something else," Rosie said when the door shut behind them.

"That man, selling your house, your quilts. He is a bad man," said Auntie Palu.

"Aunt Etta says there is no way to stop him," Rosie said.

"This war is changing the island. The aloha spirit, it is disappearing in the smoke of the bombs," Auntie Palu said. She handed Rosie the quilt. "Leilani and I are on our way to the Army base to serve the boys refreshments and aloha spirit. We must not let this war take it away from us. Rosie, you must come with us! Leilani, invite Rosie to come to the army base with us."

"I can't today, Auntie Palu. I have to watch Freddie."

"Auntie Palu!" Freddie called. He waved wildly.

"My Freddie! I have missed you!" Auntie Palu caught Freddie as he flew across the street and she covered his face with kisses.

"Rosie and I are detectives. We're on a stakeout watching

for Mr. Smith to sell some of our stuff," he said. "Hey, you have a quilt!"

"It's one of Mama's," Rosie said. "One Auntie Palu made."

"No, you two must let the authorities take care of bad men," Auntie Palu scolded Rosie and Freddie. "Tell your Aunt Etta what is happening."

"She has so much on her mind," Rosie said. "And I want proof of what is going on so when Mama and Papa return, they can do something about Mr. Smith."

"Dear girl, I don't know. You need to be careful," said Auntie Palu.

"I will. Promise."

"Who is the boy across the street watching you?" Leilani elbowed Rosie.

"That's Kam. He's a friend."

"He's going to teach us to surf," said Freddie.

Leilani waved her fingers at Kam, smiling and batting her eyes.

Rosie elbowed her back.

"I'm just having fun," said Leilani. "He's your boyfriend."

"No!" said Rosie. "He's our *friend*."

"We are late!" Auntie Palu said, walking quickly toward her car. "Next time, Roselie, you will come to help us with the Army boys."

"I will be in touch. I miss you!" Leilani gave Rosie a quick hug then ran to catch up with her mother who was already halfway down the block.

Rosie hugged the quilt to her.

"So that's it?" Kam said.

Rosie nodded.

"We don't have to follow Mr. Smith anymore, right?" said Freddie as they walked toward home.

"I think we know what happened to the things from our house," said Rosie. But, she thought, that is only half the mystery of her parents' internment. She still didn't know who had reported on them or why. That would have to wait until another day.

Chapter 28

Rosie sat outside on the stoop when they returned from following Mr. Smith. She had carefully recorded their adventure, names, places, and dates, in her journal and tucked the quilt away on a top shelf of the closet. She would bring it out at the right moment to surprise Aunt Etta.

And Leilani was her friend again. This was the best day in a long time.

Rosie hoped, after the day they'd had, that Aunt Etta would bring home something good from the food stand where she worked. She was not in the mood to eat coconut again.

There was a cooling breeze off the ocean and except for the barbed wire, a nice view of the water. Rosie realized that she was humming along with Hawaiian music drifting across the yard from the house next door. She'd thought that house was empty.

"Aloha!" a woman's voice called as Rosie stood and stretched, trying to see who was playing music so loud she could hear it across the yards.

A youngish woman, maybe about Aunt Etta's age, stood in the middle of the yard with two small children and they all swayed to the music. The woman had long dark hair with a red flower tucked behind one ear and wore a fitted flowered dress. "Join us," she said, motioning gracefully for Rosie to come.

Hula dancer, Rosie thought, and the small girls were imitating her every move.

"I'm Iolana," she said, still dancing. "We moved in last night. Do you by any chance babysit?"

"For my brother," Rosie said, not able to take her eyes off the dancer. Not only did she dance well, but she was also beautiful in an exotic way. Living on the beach brought something new every day. And this neighborhood was more "authentic" Hawaiian than anyplace she'd ever lived.

"Is there any chance you'd want to earn some extra money by watching a few more kids?"

Rosie knew they could use the extra money. "I should probably ask my aunt."

"Not every day," the woman continued.

"My mother used to run a kindergarten," Rosie said, warming to the idea.

"Then you are perfect!" Iolana said.

"Rosie?" Aunt Etta called as she came up the sandy path to their house.

"Over here! We have neighbors."

Iolana shooed the children off to play and reached inside the house and turned the record player down. "Your aunt?"

Rosie nodded as Aunt Etta crossed the dirt lawn and joined them. She quickly introduced the two women.

"I was trying to talk your niece into helping us out over here," Iolana said. "I need some babysitting while I work."

"If Rosie wants to. At least until school starts again." Aunt Etta looked at Rosie.

"Okay," Rosie agreed. "When do I start?" Maybe she could make enough money to buy a dress to wear when school did resume. And a bathing suit. She missed swimming but she had nothing to wear. Rosie promised to go over around nine a.m. the next day to watch Iolana's two small girls.

"I have a surprise for your birthday," Etta said, as they walked back toward the house.

"Food?" Rosie said. Please let it be food! "A cake?" She'd almost forgotten her birthday was coming up on Sunday. She figured there would be no presents and certainly no party.

"No, no. Though I do have a few cheese sandwiches tonight. Mr. Peters gave them to me and I didn't even have to sneak them off someone's plate. I think he feels bad for paying me so little. And I have chips, too. They are kind of smushed up but they will taste the same. But that isn't the surprise." Aunt Etta faced Rosie and took her hands. "Your mother has been moved to Sand Island and that means we can go visit!"

Rosie squeezed her aunt's hands. "They won't lie and say

she isn't there? We'll truly see her?" Since Aunt Etta had returned, it had been easier to deal with missing Mama and Papa. But with the possibility she might see them soon, it flooded over her how much she wanted to.

"Your mother," Aunt Etta cautioned. "Your papa is still with the rest of the men on the mainland. I think they were near San Francisco but I've heard they are moving again."

"That's really far," said Rosie, her lower lip quivering.

"Your mama will tell you all about it. Sunday. We are going on your birthday."

"And I have a new job to keep me busy until then," Rosie said. She felt excitement plant itself in her stomach, but didn't want to let it grow too big. There had been too many disappointments and letting herself get too excited only made the disappointment worse.

"You are a good, good girl, you know it? I am very happy I don't have to worry about you and Freddie so long as you're in charge."

Rosie wondered what her aunt would think if she knew they had been spending time spying on Mr. Smith. In fact, she decided this might not be the time to tell her about what they had seen today or show her the quilt, with things going well for now. Aunt Etta hadn't looked so happy since the last time George had stopped by. She was normally tense and worried these days, so Rosie decided to let her enjoy looking forward to their visit to Sand Island.

Sand Island. It sounded lovely.

Chapter 29

"I worked last night and need to sleep awhile," Iolana said when Rosie came over the next morning. She was still dressed in a flowered top and "grass" skirt and wore wilting leis around her neck. The leis smelled lovely despite their brown edges. "The girls will be happy to play outside and I'll be up by lunchtime. My mother stays with them at night but she has to work, too."

"I'll keep them quiet," Rosie promised, smiling at the two small girls who looked remarkably alike sitting on the couch eating bread and jam.

"Girls, listen to Rosie and behave!" Iolana said sternly as she disappeared into the back of the house.

"Let's finish your breakfast outside," Rosie said. She didn't want to mess up her first day and have the girls keep Iolana from sleeping. Although they hadn't said a word yet.

It didn't take long for them to start talking and when they started, they didn't stop. Once Rosie knew their names, she quickly discovered the rest of their story—they were twins, their dad was in the Navy, they loved the water, dancing, and make believe.

The girls, Daisy and Merigold, were easy enough to watch. They had an entire repertoire of pretend games that only involved the two of them. Rosie sat on the steps and watched. She thought perhaps the next time she was needed she might bring a book or her quilt square along.

"Hey, we all have flowery names," Daisy said, seating herself on the step beside Rosie.

"We do."

"Our mom likes flowers," said Merigold. "When we have a house where we live by ourselves, we are going to have a flower garden."

"That's nice."

"Do you know how to hula?" Merigold asked.

"I don't," said Rosie.

"But you're Hawaiian! All of us know how to hula," said Daisy.

Rosie lifted her dark hair off her neck. Hmm, mistaken again for Hawaiian. It had to be her deepening tan and the way she held her hair out of her face with braided ti leaves. She pushed away the feeling she was being disloyal to her German heritage and felt relieved it was so easy to deceive people. "Never learned," Rosie said.

"We can teach you! We are very good dancers!" Daisy pulled on Rosie's hand.

Maybe it was time to learn the hula. She and Freddie could have their own act—he could play ukulele and she would dance the hula.

"Learn how to do some dance moves, then we will play a record. Mama says you can't find good Hawaiian tunes on the radio," said Daisy.

The girls made it look so easy, but it took Rosie awhile to relax enough to let her body move freely.

"Think about the breeze and how it moves through the trees," said Daisy.

"And how the fish swim through the water," Merigold added.

"And the waves meeting the sand," Daisy said.

Rosie remembered one of the songs she had heard the Palus play again and again, thought about what the girls had told her, and closed her eyes. Her body seemed to float.

She heard applause and when Rosie opened her eyes, Iolana leaned against the doorway, wearing a silk robe tied tightly at the waist and smoking a cigarette. "Very nice," she said, grinning, "if you want to earn some more money, you can come to the club with me and teach the soldiers to dance. Every single one of them wants to learn to hula."

"Your girls are good teachers!" said Rosie. "I didn't think I could do it, but they kept giving me hints and now, well, I'm at least not embarrassed like I was at the very beginning."

"They are quite the little dancers."

"Rosie got better when we told her about the breeze and the fish and the waves," said Daisy, who Rosie had noticed was always first to speak.

Iolana smiled at her girls, then turned to Rosie. "It always feels awkward at first but you looked good." She disappeared inside for a moment and then music drifted out of the house. "Listen to the music and let the notes carry your arms and your hips." She swayed gently to the beat. "Go ahead. Try it. Don't think about your body, think about the music."

Rosie closed her eyes again, partly because she didn't want to see the expressions on the faces of anyone who happened to be watching. She listened for a moment then swayed, added some arm movements, then moved her hips the way the girls had showed her. It was feeling better.

She heard clapping again and opened her eyes. Kam was watching from her yard. She stopped mid-move. How embarrassing for him to show up now!

"I came to give Freddie a surfing lesson. Heard there were good waves today," he said.

"Your boyfriend?" Iolana asked, grinning.

"No, no!" Rosie said, feeling herself blush all over. "He's a friend, teaching my brother to surf."

"He's very cute," teased Iolana. "You need to eat if you are going to surf all afternoon. Want to join us for lunch?"

"I'm not surfing. Just Freddie. I've—I haven't got—I

outgrew my bathing suit and haven't had a chance to buy a new one," Rosie said quickly, wishing she didn't have to lie.

"A bathing suit? I have many. You can borrow one of them until you have a chance to shop. So, lunch?"

Lunch? She and Freddie usually skipped lunch unless there was food left over from the night before. And there wasn't a bite left for them today. But could she eat and leave Freddie out? And there was Kam, waiting for them.

"Thanks, but . . ."

"Call your brother to join us," Iolana offered. "And you, surfer boy, come have a bite of lunch with us!" Iolana had such a kind look on her face, Rosie wondered if she knew how little they had to eat in their house. "It won't be much," the woman said, "just some bread and butter."

Rosie's mouth watered. It didn't take much these days.

"I've already had lunch," Kam said, joining them in front of Iolana's house. He rested his surfboard against her porch. "But I'll provide some musical entertainment." He held up the ukulele.

The twins each grabbed one of Kam's arms and led him into the house, talking away.

Rosie called Freddie away from his pals and they joined Kam, Iolana, and her twins at the kitchen table.

"I am so happy to have such nice neighbors!" Iolana said. "Some of my friends haven't been so lucky! There's this one girl I know whose mother overheard her employer speaking with her husband in German, planning who knows what, and she turned them in to the FBI, said they were Nazis. I mean, everybody knows that Nazis speak German." Iolana nodded to emphasize how she felt.

Rosie hung her head. Nazis spoke German, but not everyone who spoke German was a Nazi.

"But," Iolana continued, "my friend also said that her mother ended up with her boss's job. So who knows why she really turned her in." She shrugged.

Rosie stiffened. The story had a familiar ring to it. Malia had ended up with her mother's business and their house. She fought the idea, but it was looking more likely that Malia could be the "who" that had reported on her parents.

Freddie stood up. "Kam, are you still going to surf with me?"

Kam also stood and nodded.

"I should stay and help with the dishes," Rosie offered, although she hoped that Iolana would refuse. She needed to get away. She wanted to write in her journal.

"Oh, no! Thank you so much for taking good care of the girls. Practice your dancing and I'll give you more pointers next time. I'll teach you how to tell a story." Iolana moved her arms as she sat at the table.

"Thank you for the lunch," said Rosie.

"Thank you," Freddie echoed.

"But Kam didn't play his ukulele," said Merigold.

"Next time. Teach Rosie a dance and I will play and she will dance," he said.

"Wait a minute. I promised to lend you a bathing suit." Iolana disappeared into the back room and returned almost immediately, holding a navy blue one-piece suit by the strap. "I think this will fit." Then, she pulled her purse off the kitchen cabinet and searched through it finally handing Rosie a dollar bill.

Rosie tried to hand it back. "This is too much with lunch and the suit."

Iolana refused to take it. "Nothing is too much to make sure my girls are well cared for," she said. "Like I said, I'm so glad to have good neighbors."

A dollar! Rosie stared at the crisp new bill. Across the back of it was printed HAWAII. Rosie had read how all the old paper money had to be turned in to the government and burned. That money was replaced with special war money. If the island was invaded, the government would declare the HAWAII money no good and the Japs would have no money to spend.

"Hey," said Kam, elbowing her gently in the side, "treats are on you."

"I will let you know when we need you again. And thanks again," said Iolana.

Rosie followed Kam and Freddie out of the house.

"I'll take your brother down to the beach while you change. Then, I'll teach you both to ride the waves." Kam grinned.

Rosie felt exhausted—the new job, the money, what Iolana had said about people being encouraged to report Germans,

Italians, and Japanese and her hint that some made the reports for their own benefit. She'd thought no matter how wrong it might be, the informers believed they had something real to report. Now she wasn't so sure their motives—M-O-T-I-V-E-S—were always pure.

Rosie looked out at the waves breaking on the beach. It had been so long since she'd had a good cleansing swim and maybe that was what she needed to clear her mind before she wrote anything in her journal. She nodded at Kam and turned toward the house as he and Freddie headed for the beach.

The bathing suit fit fairly well and Rosie wrapped a towel around her before leaving the house. The sand felt particularly hot on her bare feet as she made her way through the opening in the barbed wire to the beach. Kam and Freddie were goofing off in the shallow water and waved when they saw her.

When she was under the open sky of the beach, Rosie checked first that there were no planes overhead and then she listened to make sure she heard no sirens. When she was certain it was safe, she dropped the towel and ran quickly into the water. It felt even better than she'd imagined.

Rosie spent the entire afternoon in the ocean with only short breaks on the sand. When Kam said he had to go or his auntie would be worried, she couldn't believe how quickly the time had gone.

Aunt Etta was already home when Rosie went inside. Freddie was telling her about the bread and butter lunch

Iolana had served them. When Rosie joined them, he left to change his clothes.

"You've been swimming," Aunt Etta said.

Rosie nodded. "Iolana, from next door, lent me this suit."

"I should have realized that you didn't have one!" said her aunt. "Living here on the beach and you with no swimsuit. Iolana is turning out to be the best thing to happen around here in a while."

"You are the best thing to happen to us," said Rosie, again so grateful to Aunt Etta for rescuing them from Aunt Yvonne.

"I'm going to march with my company," Freddie said as he ran out the door.

Aunt Etta shook her head. "I hope this war doesn't last long enough that he has to become a real soldier. Bad enough that George might have to go!"

"George!"

"Not yet. But the possibility is always there. Just as I may, for whatever reason, be sent back to the internment camp."

Aunt Etta leaned back against the sofa and closed her eyes.

"I have something to tell you and something to ask," Rosie said. "I've been thinking about informers today."

Aunt Etta sighed.

"Before you came to us the first time, the government men searching our house asked me about your photos hanging on the wall. I told them you took the pictures, the ones of Pearl Harbor and Germany. I didn't mean to inform on you, but was that . . . could that . . ."

Aunt Etta shook her head. "I don't know why I was interned. Most of us didn't know a reason why. It could have been the photos, although I'm sure the FBI knew about them way before you told them. Also, I had been to Germany recently with George. Please don't worry yourself that you had anything to do with me being interned."

If she knew why Aunt Etta had been interned, Rosie thought it would be easier not to worry about what she had said.

"Then let me ask you something else."

Again, her aunt sighed.

"You know how you said, well not just you said it, that sometimes people made reports to the FBI about Germans, and other . . ." Rosie had to hesitate a moment before saying the hated words, "enemy aliens or plain old enemies?"

"That reporting didn't start yesterday," said Aunt Etta.

"I know that. But my question is, what if the reporting person benefits if the German or Italian or Japanese are taken away? Like Malia. If she turned Mama and Papa in claiming it was because she heard them speak German, or because of Papa's radios, it could have been more because she wanted them out of the way so she could have the kindergarten again."

"It could have happened that way," Aunt Etta said, her eyes remaining closed. "But we will never know."

"But what if we report on Malia? Tell the government men that Malia was lying because she wanted the kindergarten for herself?" Rosie said.

"I don't think so," said Aunt Etta, still not looking at Rosie.

"Why not? She lied!" Rosie said, starting to get mad at Aunt Etta as well as Malia.

Aunt Etta shook her head. "No one will listen. Darling, now it's different days and no matter who says it, who they say it about, the government takes all the reports seriously."

"So anyone can say anything about anybody and that person will be interned?"

"There are exceptions. I myself have been accused and interned. The officials wouldn't take my word for anything. They think I'm a traitor."

Rosie watched tears roll down her aunt's face.

"But, but . . ." Rosie hesitated trying to form her words, "that isn't the way it's supposed to be. Don't we have rights?"

Aunt Etta shook her head again. "Martial law."

Rosie shivered in cold fear. "They could really take you away again?"

"I would hope not, but yes, I could be interned again, like before, like your Mama and Papa."

At that thought, Rosie grew cold. And, she realized, her aunt was right. They couldn't do anything that might damage their already risky position.

Rosie ran out of the room and threw herself across the bed. Internment was wrong, and confusing, and scary. She hated the war. She hated these different days.

Chapter 30

The two days until January 11th—her birthday and their visit to Sand Island—seemed an eternity. It had been almost five weeks since she'd seen Mama and the waiting was excruciating. E-X-C-R-U-C-I-A-T-I-N-G. Words from her spelling list still popped into her mind.

When the morning finally came, she washed her hair and asked Aunt Etta to please braid it. She had washed and pressed the dress Leilani had given her and it fit perfectly. Rosie squeezed her feet into her too-small shoes.

Freddie was so excited about seeing Mama, neither Rosie nor her aunt could settle him down enough to convince him to change his clothes. When it came time to run for the bus they were taking to the dock, he still looked like he'd just climbed out of bed.

At the dock, Rosie followed Aunt Etta onto a small

launch driven by a soldier. Freddie moved until he was as close to the military man as he could sit and started asking questions. The launch was crowded with family members of internees. No one spoke to anyone else and most didn't even look at one another. The thing that she did notice was that they didn't look any different than she looked, or most of the people she met on the street looked. And yet, each one must be hiding the same big secret she was. Were they as afraid as she was? What if once she reached the camp, she would be made to stay? One minute she wanted the boat to go faster and the next she wasn't sure she wanted to arrive on the island at all.

As they walked across a field of white coral, Rosie heard what sounded like a chorus of crying. She held tightly to Aunt Etta's hand while Freddie ran ahead, waited for them, and then ran ahead again. What was the sound?

As soon as the camp came into sight, she knew. Women, many Japanese and fewer *haole*, stood behind the tall barbed wire fences with their arms poked through the wire, crying and calling for their family members. It was such an eerie sound, it gave Rosie a creepy feeling. The guard towers looming over them contributed to the feeling.

A woman wearing a guard uniform met them at the entrance and led the group to a large dining hall filled with tables and benches. Mama appeared as if by magic, her arms held wide. Rosie ran to her and leaned in, her mother's arm pulling her tightly against her. There were no words.

Even when Mama let go and pushed Rosie away to look at her better, she said, Rosie couldn't say anything. She stared and stared, making sure it was still her same mama. It was.

"You've grown! Your hair is longer and you are so tanned!" Mama marveled.

"I've grown too. And we live near the beach so we play outside all the time. I'm learning to be a soldier!" Freddie did all the talking. "And how to surf and how to play the ukulele."

Mama stroked Freddie's hair, smoothing it and making it lay down. "Yes, you have grown, too!" She pulled him close and kissed him all over his face.

"Mama! Soldiers don't let their mamas kiss them like that!" He wiped his face.

Rosie laughed. "He plays army so much, he will be a general before this war is over."

Mama shook her head. "I hope it doesn't last that long!"

Rosie took a quick look around the room. People sat in tight knots, talking, kissing, holding hands and sometimes simply staring at one another. She felt a stab of fear when her gaze landed on the guards standing at each doorway, their eyes moving back and forth over the internees and their visitors. The windows were all painted over, making it dark inside the room, but the space around Mama looked brighter than anyplace else in the room. Aunt Etta had taken off to greet some of the women she had met when she was interned at Fort Armstrong.

"Do you sleep in here?" Freddie asked.

"In a barracks," Mama answered. "Some people sleep in tents."

"Where's Papa? I thought we would see Papa," Freddie said, his eyes suddenly filling with tears.

"Papa is in a different camp. I hope he will return soon," Mama said, her voice ragged.

"Can you come home with us?" Freddie asked, grasping her hand.

"Not today, my brave soldier," Mama said. "Let us talk of cheerier things. Rosie, I have a surprise for you! I will be right back." She smiled broadly and hurried away.

Rosie didn't want to let her go for even a minute. She watched until Mama disappeared behind a door, then kept her eyes glued to that door waiting for her mama to come back.

She caught her breath when the door opened. Mama carried a beautifully decorated cake with candles blazing. People turned as she walked past and soon someone started singing, "Happy birthday to you . . ."

Rosie barely heard, all her attention on the cake. There was a birthday cake for her!

"I hope it's chocolate," Freddie said. "Make a wish! Blow out the candles!"

Rosie closed her eyes and wished for what she knew could not happen—that Mama return home with them. She opened her eyes and blew. One candle remained ablaze. Freddie blew it out for her.

"You won't believe who baked this cake for you," Mama

said as she set it down on the table. A large woman, wearing a white apron and a tall chef's hat had followed Mama, carrying a knife and a stack of plates.

Mama grabbed the woman's arm and pulled her toward Rosie. "This is Elisabeta and she is the pastry chef at the Grand Waikiki Hotel."

"Ja, they think I will add poison to all the food we serve the generals so they lock me up here where I cook for all my friends," Elisabeta said with a laugh.

Some of the other women joined in the laughter although Mama's smile seemed forced.

"Thank you for the cake. It's beautiful," said Rosie. The cake was frosted in swirls of white and decorated with flowers in many bright colors. She almost hated to see it cut into but her mouth watered with anticipation of the sweetness.

Elisabeta cut into the cake and gave Rosie the first piece.

"Me next," Freddie pushed forward, "I'm the birthday girl's favorite brother."

Everyone laughed at Freddie as he took his cake and sat beside Rosie.

Mama sat across from them and stared while they ate. "Don't you want a piece?" Rosie asked.

Mama shook her head. "I eat Elisabeta's food all the time. So, you can see it's not that bad. And I want to hear all about you. What about your new house?"

Rosie let Freddie describe the house and he made it sound much better than she would have.

"We have a nice neighbor," said Rosie. "I watch her daughters for her in the mornings. They're twins."

"Ah! Here comes Etta! Is she taking good care of you?" Mama asked as Etta joined them on the bench.

"She's the best!" said Rosie.

"Are you having a good birthday?" Aunt Etta asked.

"The best," said Rosie. She wished she could take a piece of the cake to Kam. She couldn't wait to tell him who had baked her birthday cake.

"Look, they are putting out sandwiches. Freddie, Rosie, would you go grab a few of them before they are all gone?" Mama pointed toward a table with trays of sandwiches lined up. People were already helping themselves.

"I'll go. One, two, three, four. Right?" said Freddie.

"Rosie, go with him," Mama said.

Rosie didn't want to go. She didn't want to waste even one minute of her time with Mama. Besides, she was full of cake. She walked slowly away.

"I heard from Mr. Smith, the man handling our property," Rosie heard Mama say. Rosie walked even more slowly, listening hard.

"He wants to sell our Diamond Head property, says he can't pay the taxes and it may be foreclosed upon. Would you check into it for me, please? I've written to the loan company to inform them we don't want to sell," Mama said.

"Mr. Smith told us he couldn't give us an allowance because all the money is going toward paying the cost of keeping the property," Aunt Etta said, her face reddening. "He's given us nothing! And he said we couldn't live in the Diamond Head house because he'd rented it. The taxes couldn't be that much!"

"I wish I knew what was going on," said Mama.

Rosie knew. Mr. Smith was robbing them of everything! If she told Mama, it would ruin their entire visit, not to mention how angry Aunt Etta would be to find out that they'd spied on Mr. Smith.

"Ham sandwiches!" Freddie ran down the aisle holding them in the air.

"How wonderful!" Mama said.

"They are so good," said Freddie, talking with his mouth full.

Rosie ate hers slowly. She hadn't had ham since they left Aunt Yvonne's and it tasted delicious.

When Freddie had finished, Mama handed him her sandwich. "I eat all the time," she said. "You can have it."

Rosie didn't believe her for a minute. Mama was thinner than she'd ever been.

Aunt Etta held hers out to Rosie.

"I'm full," said Rosie, patting her stomach, knowing that Aunt Etta hadn't eaten much lately either.

"Rosie is learning the hula," said Freddie.

"You are?" Mama looked like she didn't believe it.

"That's Iolana's job, hula dancer. And the girls are really good at dancing, too. They thought I was Hawaiian and that it was a shame I didn't know the hula," Rosie said. "And I'm learning to quilt. Kealani, who worked for Aunt Yvonne, started teaching me, but I'm working by myself on the quilt square she gave me."

"I wish I had my quilting to work on!" Mama said. "I hope Mr. Smith has all of our things stored in a safe place. It worries me."

And it should, thought Rosie, still not willing to ruin their time together by saying anything of what she'd seen spying on Mr. Smith.

"Rosie is bringing in extra money babysitting. It has been a great help. *She* is a great help," Aunt Etta said.

Rosie sat up a little taller, warmed by her aunt's words.

The rest of the visit passed quickly, too quickly, and Rosie found herself back on the launch crossing the water before she knew it. She waved and waved until her arm hurt and Sand Island had vanished in the distance.

Despite the barbed wire and the rows of tents, the darkened windows in the mess hall and the guards, Sand Island was beautiful, Rosie decided, if only because Mama was there.

Chapter 31

School finally resumed in mid-January. So many of the buildings had been taken over for use by the military that the remaining buildings were overcrowded and students attended in shifts. Rosie and Freddie drew the afternoon shift.

Rosie was glad because she could still take care of Daisy and Merigold. Aunt Etta had insisted from the beginning that she keep a quarter of every dollar she earned. She said Rosie could save it, spend it, or if she was very, very hungry, eat it. Rosie had saved every single penny. When she heard that school would start, she spent every penny on a new dress.

Rosie and Kam chose seats near one another in their new classroom.

"Were there this many kids in your class before?" Rosie asked as she looked at the desks crowded together in the classroom. She was so close to Kam and the girls in front of and behind her that she felt like she had to press her arms against her sides to keep from spreading into their space.

"Nope," said Kam. "And there are a lot of people here I've never seen before."

A young Hawaiian woman rushed into the room and stood behind the teacher's desk. She gripped the wooden chair tightly and smiled at the class. "I'm Miss Akana and I will be your teacher." She took a deep breath.

Rosie wondered if she had ever taught before, she seemed so nervous. Her hair was in a messy bun at the back of her head and she wore a navy blue skirt and jacket with white trim. She had to be hot in a jacket. Rosie was sweating in her sleeveless dress and bare feet. Miss Akana also wore high-heeled shoes. Rosie's teacher at her old school had never looked this nice.

Miss Akana called the roll, struggling with the Japanese names.

"Call 'em all Tojo," a boy's voice said from the back of the room.

Miss Akana looked up and around quickly. "Who said that?"

The room fell silent.

Rosie braced for what the other students might say when Miss Akana called her very German name.

"In this classroom, we will respect one another," the teacher said firmly and continued calling the roll by first name only. It didn't change knowing which kids were Japanese, but

Rosie was relieved not to have her secret revealed. She liked this teacher.

At recess, Kam joined a game of baseball and Rosie stood by as a group of girls jumped rope. She wished Betty was here to play with but she went to a nearby Catholic school.

"You want a turn?" a girl she thought was named Apikalia asked her.

As Rosie shook her head, one of the Japanese girls answered, "I do."

"Catch the next bomber back to Japan," Apikalia said.

The Japanese girl backed up a few steps and swiped at her eyes. She turned and Rosie touched her arm. "Don't pay any attention to her," she said. "We'll find our own jumprope."

The girl tried to smile. "I'm Haruko," she said.

"Rosie."

"You'd better watch what you say around the Japs," Apikalia yelled at Rosie's back. "Open trap make happy Jap."

"Don't pay any attention to them," Rosie called to Haruko, who was walking swiftly away.

Before Rosie could catch up to her, the bell rang and Haruko ran to the schoolhouse door.

Kam caught up with Rosie and as he always did, punched her in the arm. "You didn't make any friends today," he said in a whisper.

Rosie glanced over her shoulder at Apikalia and the group of Hawaiian girls standing together staring in her direction. Apikalia glared at her.

"I did make a friend. Haruko," Rosie said.

"*She* will help you fit in," Kam said with a sniff.

Rosie walked away from him and took her seat, surprised at Kam's words. He'd never seemed prejudiced against her, a German, but his lack of prejudice didn't seem to extend to Japanese. She opened a book and stared at the page in front of her but saw nothing. She hated what the war had done to her family, taking Mama and Papa away, labeling them enemy aliens when they'd done nothing wrong—just because they were German. Yet, it had to be worse to be Japanese. Haruko and the other Japanese kids were judged on the way they looked. She glanced at Kam talking and laughing with the boy seated on his other side. At least no one in school but him knew about her family. She was determined to keep it that way and equally determined to make sure she didn't reject Haruko just because she was Japanese.

When Rosie finished her math assignment, she pulled out her journal and wrote, *There is a mix of kids at this new school. The Hawaiian kids say mean things to the Japanese and I bet they would say mean things to me if they knew my parents were German and interned.*

"Rosie?" Miss Akana stopped beside her desk.

Rosie looked up and shut her journal.

"Are you writing in a journal?" the teacher asked.

Rosie nodded, hoping she wouldn't take it away.

"It's a good thing to record your thoughts about what is

happening these days," Miss Akana said with a smile. "By the way, your spelling test was 100 percent correct."

Spelling. Rosie had almost forgotten about the spelling bee she had so looked forward to at her former school. "Miss Akana, do you think this school will be taking part in the All-Island spelling championship?"

Miss Akana looked thoughtful. "I'm not sure I know about that."

"At my other school, I was one of the finalists—" Rosie spoke quickly, "in the spelling bee. I mean, I'm sure this school has already picked their finalists, too, but maybe . . ."

"So she's a Jap lover and a spelling champion," Rosie heard someone, Apikalia she suspected, whisper loudly. "La-dee-da!"

"I will check into it and if there is to be a spelling bee, I'm sure we can make adjustments to who participates," Miss Akana said.

Rosie sat back, feeling excited about the spelling bee again. At least the possibility. She might become a champion yet.

Chapter 32

"George is stopping by this evening," Aunt Etta said after they had eaten supper and Rosie was settled at the kitchen table doing homework.

"He's been really busy, hasn't he?" Rosie said. "You want me to take my things in the bedroom and finish?"

"He is busy, and no, you don't have to go in the other room," her aunt said as the screen door screeched open.

"Aloha!" George stepped inside. Aunt Etta greeted him with a kiss. "We need to oil those hinges!"

"The squeaking will give us notice if any Japs try to invade our house," Aunt Etta teased.

"Newspapers," George said, throwing a pile on the sofa. He sprawled in the orange easy chair and it also creaked miserably. "Guess they won't invade this chair either."

Aunt Etta sat on the arm of the chair, leaning against him.

"I asked about doing a feature story on Sand Island and the editor said no, a firm no. He said no one should even know what is going on there," George said, his head back and eyes closed. "I don't know what else to do. Now, I hear that on the mainland all Japanese who live in areas that have been designated military zones will be relocated inland because of the threat they pose."

"Here in Hawaii too?" Rosie asked.

"We rely too heavily on Japanese labor here in Hawaii," George said, "or that's what they say. That's also why they aren't relocating the Germans on the mainland. Or that's what I'm told."

"Did you find out anything about Mr. Smith? He's threatening to sell more of their property," Aunt Etta said.

"I've been talking to a friend, Will Weinstein, who is in the property business," George said. "He doesn't think much of our Mr. Smith."

"He's selling more than just houses," Rosie said.

Both Aunt Etta and George looked at her.

"I saw him take a box of jewelry to a jewelry store and come out with bills he stuck in his pocket. He also sold some quilts, including one of Mama's that Auntie Palu made for her. Auntie Palu bought it back." Rosie ran into the bedroom and brought out the quilt. She tossed it across their laps.

"What do you mean, you 'saw' him?" Aunt Etta asked in her sternest voice. She examined the quilt, looking from it to Rosie.

Rosie couldn't bear to see the expression on her aunt's face. "When we saw our lamp in his office, both of us, Freddie and me, we knew he was up to no good." Rosie shrugged again. "So we've kind of been keeping an eye on him."

"You dragged your brother into this?!" Aunt Etta said, her voice shrill.

When Rosie dared to glance up, she saw Aunt Etta glaring at her. "Freddie thought we were playing a detective game. And Mr. Smith never saw me," she assured her aunt. "And it was only two times."

"And what do you plan to do with this information?" Aunt Etta demanded.

Rosie had seldom seen her aunt so angry. She wished she hadn't said anything, but how could she keep quiet when someone was stealing from her family. "I don't know really," Rosie finally answered. "I figured, being German and all, no one would believe me, but just in case I wanted to be able to give proof. I kept notes on everything I've seen Mr. Smith do."

"May I see your notes?" George asked reasonably.

"They're in my journal," Rosie said.

"Still, if I can give Will a timeline, something he can work with, perhaps he can come up with a way to stop the man. IF, and this is a big if, he is doing anything illegal. These days, it would be very hard to prove," George said.

I-L-L-E-G-A-L, Rosie spelled to herself. "What if I think the reason my parents were interned is illegal?" she asked.

"Rosie," Aunt Etta said sharply.

"Now, Etta, some would agree with Rosie that the concept of internment is illegal. Seems like our Rosie has been having deep thoughts."

"Let's say the person who reported on Mama and Papa exaggerated," Rosie paused and spelled E-X-A-G-G-E-R-A-T-E-D to herself. "Or even lied about their activities, because they wanted something those people had. Like Malia."

George looked at Aunt Etta and frowned.

"George, we can't make accusations like that," said Aunt Etta, looking frightened. "They'll never believe us. And it means, it means I'll be back on their radar. I don't want to risk being locked up again and leaving the children. Rosie, you have to understand. I'm not trying to be difficult. There are so many ways to look at this!"

Rosie felt a surge of anger at her aunt. She was too afraid to do anything, to say anything.

Freddie burst into the living room. "Hey, George, want to come see us march? There's a real soldier who has been work-ing with us and we look as good as his real unit—he said so!"

"I bet you do!" said George.

"Tomorrow, Freddie. It's time for you and Rosie to go to bed. Morning will be here before you know it. And you need to wash your face, hands, and feet." Aunt Etta placed her hands on Freddie's shoulders and pushed him toward the bedroom.

Rosie was willing to go to bed. She was afraid of what she might say, feeling as mad as she felt. It wasn't Aunt Etta's home that might be sold, or her quilts, or her furniture or anything of hers. Aunt Etta hadn't lost the pet she'd had ever since she could remember. Rosie gathered the newspapers George had brought to read before she fell asleep.

Aunt Etta tried to put her arm around Rosie but Rosie pulled away. "Don't think we aren't doing anything or don't care," her aunt said. "George is working every day to free your parents and to keep their property from being sold."

"I just hope you can do something before it's too late." Rosie turned to follow Freddie to bed, not taking time to kiss her aunt good night.

Chapter 33

Before school the next day, Rosie found a piece of clothesline under the sink at Iolana's house and asked her neighbor if she could use it for a jumprope. At school, she invited Haruko and several other Japanese and *haole* girls to jump with her. Only one of the *haole* girls joined them, but she and Haruko and a few of Haruko's friends ate lunch together. It felt good to have friends at school.

Haruko and Rosie were turning the rope as Annette, a girl from the fifth grade, jumped. A line of other girls waited for her to miss so they could take her place. A boy, smaller than Freddie, pulled on Haruko's arm, making the rope jerk and Annette's feet grow tangled.

"Not fair!" Annette yelled. "It's not my fault I missed."

Haruko had dropped her end of the rope and moved to the edge of the playground, her arm around the little boy.

His shoulders shook with sobs as they talked. Haruko tried to comfort him but finally led him, still crying, into the school building.

The girl at the end of the line took up Haruko's end and turned with Rosie. When recess ended and Rosie and the rest of the class came inside, Haruko wasn't there.

"Miss Akana?" Rosie asked when the dismissal bell rang. "What happened to Haruko? Was that her brother crying?"

Miss Akana nodded. "She took him home. Aki wouldn't stop crying." She shook her head.

"But what happened?"

Miss Akana looked at Rosie, chewing on her lower lip. "I'm sorry but Haruko needs to tell you that herself."

"Can you tell me where she lives?"

"I'm afraid I can't. And shouldn't you be heading home? Your mother will be worried."

"Will she be back tomorrow?" Rosie asked.

"Probably." Miss Akana smiled at Rosie. "I have some good news for you. We are going to have a spelling bee. The faculty decided we'd start from scratch and let anyone interested take part. I'm hoping you will."

"I will. I've been practicing words. I'm so glad!" Rosie nodded, punctuating her words.

Miss Akana smiled warmly. "I'll keep you informed."

"Thank you," Rosie said as she backed out of the room. "Thanks!"

Heading home, Rosie wondered if Miss Akana would be

willing to help with her application to Punahou. Maybe it was time to think about the future.

The walk home was unusually quiet. Freddie and Kam had gone ahead, planning to fish at a place Kam had found. The two of them had a new passion for catching fish and splitting the catch between their two families for dinner. It beat coconuts any day and it kept Freddie busy as he had deserted army play for now to go with Kam.

Rosie looked forward to time on her own. She had made great progress on her quilt square. She'd finished the applique work and was quilting around the edges of the fish design. She wished she could show Kealani. Rosie had sewn many positive thoughts and prayers into the square, mainly for her parents to return. And she might complete it this week if Freddie continued to fish and Iolana didn't need her to watch Daisy and Merigold. When she finished, if Kealani's prediction came true, Mama and Papa would come home.

"Three blind rats, three blind rats, Hitler, Benito, and the Jap," Rosie thought she heard someone sing. She glanced over her shoulder and saw no one, but walked a little more quickly.

"Rosie is another and so is her mother, Nazi Jap lover." The voice seemed to come from the shrubbery along the side of the road. Rosie saw no one. She felt a stab of fear and walked even more quickly.

"I know your secret," came a singsongy voice from the other side of the road.

The slithery voice reached her again, "NAAAAZIIIIII," it hissed, then laughed.

Rosie was sure whoever was taunting her was trying to disguise their voice. She broke into a run.

Chapter 34

On the way to school the next day, Rosie kept looking around her, peering into the bushes alongside the road and listening to see if anyone was following her and Freddie.

"What is going on?" Freddie asked after Rosie had turned around in a circle to see behind them for the third or fourth time.

"Nothing," she said, irritated with his questions and with herself for feeling so nervous. She had no intention of scaring her little brother.

"You are acting weird," he said. "Or maybe I should say weirder than usual."

"Oh, ha ha," said Rosie. "Hey, good fish you caught last night."

"I even know how to clean them. Cut them along the belly and pull the guts out . . ."

"Okay, okay. I get it. Well, I know how to eat them. And

luckily Aunt Etta knows how to cook them so they taste really good."

"There's Aki. See you!" Freddie started to run across the playground.

Rosie grabbed his arm. "You know Aki? Haruko's brother?"

"I don't know what his sister's name is." Freddie tried to pull away.

"Were you two playing yesterday?"

Freddie stopped and nodded.

"Why was he so upset? He came over during recess, crying, and Haruko had to take him inside."

"One of the mean kids was teasing him. Said his dad was a Tojo spy and no one should play with him, that Aki was probably a spy, too, and we should all ignore him and not talk to him." Freddie hung his head.

"Did you not play with him after that?" Rosie asked, growing angrier with every word Freddie spoke.

"Not me. He ran away before anyone could say anything. I know he's not a spy. He's a kid like me."

"You'd better hope nobody knows that we're German or they'll be saying the same things to you that they said to Aki," said Rosie, the words she'd heard on the way home the day before haunting her.

Freddie frowned. "I'm American," he said in a small voice.

"Yeah, you are," Rosie said and gave him a quick squeeze before he ran off to join his friends. Hopefully no one would think any different.

Haruko was sitting at her desk when Rosie arrived in the classroom. She was staring at a book and wouldn't look up even when Rosie spoke to her. Rosie noticed there was a folded piece of paper stuck in her desktop. She figured it was from Haruko and turned to smile at her friend, but Haruko still did not look up.

Rosie unfolded the paper.

Go back to Germany where you belong, Nazi krauthead. We don't want your kind here.

Rosie crumpled the note and looked around the room. It was definitely not from Haruko. At least she didn't think it would be something she would write. She opened her desk and dropped the note inside. The writing didn't look familiar, but the voice from yesterday didn't sound like anyone she knew either.

Who even knew about the German part of her? Besides Kam. She turned to look for her friend. He was sitting on his desktop and she figured he was talking about the fish he'd caught because he was holding his hands way farther apart than any actual fish he'd ever brought home. When he caught her looking at him, he grinned and gave a wave. It couldn't be Kam.

Rosie couldn't concentrate on the social studies lesson Miss Akana was giving about explorers or her math assignment that followed. She wanted to talk to Haruko.

At recess when Rosie followed her friend to the playground, Haruko and the rest of the Japanese girls from her class turned their backs on her and gathered in a tight circle to shut her out when she tried to talk to them. Rosie felt like she'd been punched in the stomach. The lump that had been gone for a while re-formed in her throat and she felt tears burning her eyelids but she refused to give in to them. She turned and crossed to the edge of the playground to lean against a palm tree.

The rest of the girls from her class had also formed a circle and were whispering, looking at the Japanese group, then at Rosie. Apikalia led the group in Rosie's direction. Rosie straightened up, not sure what was about to happen. The girls formed a half circle in front of her.

"Look at the alien," Apikalia taunted.

Rosie stiffened. Alien?

"Kraut!" another girl said.

"Spy!" said another.

"Hun!"

"We know your parents are locked up for being German spies. Are you in the family business?" Apikalia leaned forward, her long, dark hair rubbing against Rosie's cheek for an instant. "Nazi!"

Rosie felt hot all over. She swatted at the hair and Apikalia jerked backward. Apikalia was the one behind the note and the voice that had taunted her on the way home the day before. She was certain.

"I don't know why people like you and them—" Apikalia pointed at the group of Japanese girls, "aren't locked up. You're a danger to this country!"

"I'm as loyal to this country as you are," Rosie answered, shaking her own long, dark hair. She tried to see over the girls, to see if any teachers noticed what was happening.

"Have your parents warn Hitler we are going to pound him and all the rest of the Nazis to dust," said Apikalia.

"We aren't Nazis." Rosie felt herself growing madder and madder at being called the name she'd come to hate—and fear. She clenched her fists.

"You should be locked up with your Nazi mother and father!"

Rosie leapt forward and knocked Apikalia to the ground, screaming at her, "Take it back, take it all back! You can't call my mama and papa that name!" She straddled the girl's chest, holding her down by the shoulders and hair. Around her, Rosie could hear screams and she felt Apikalia's nails digging into her arms as she struggled, but Rosie pressed the girl harder into the warm asphalt of the playground. She wanted to push her until she disappeared and stopped calling her awful names.

"Rosie, stop it! Get off her!" She heard a boy's voice in the background and felt hands around her chest pulling at her. Rosie slapped at Apikalia as she was dragged away.

A whistle blew shrilly and Rosie saw black high heels and heard Miss Akana shout, "Rosie! Apikalia! Stop it this second." Rosie fell limp against the arms around her.

"What are you doing?" Kam whispered to her. "You are in big, big trouble."

Rosie pulled away from him but before she could take another step Miss Akana used one hand to firmly grab her by the arm while she helped Apikalia up with her other hand.

"Girls!" the teacher said, her face red and her normally perfect hair mussed. "What were you thinking?"

"She called me names, ugly names," Rosie said, using her free hand to poke her finger toward the other girl. Miss Akana held them far enough apart so Rosie couldn't touch her.

"We need to talk to Mrs. Smith right now."

Rosie felt like she'd been doused in ice water. Surely it couldn't be the same Mrs. Smith that was Aunt Yvonne's friend?

"This is the perfect way to welcome our new principal her first day at her new school. After we've all told her what wonderful students we have," Miss Akana said, sighing as she pulled them toward the building.

Rosie felt everyone staring. She looked down at her dress and noticed dirt ground into the hem as well as a tear along the waist. And it was her best dress, the one she'd bought with her babysitting money.

When they reached the office, Miss Akana sat the girls on opposite ends of the row of chairs along the wall. "Sit right here and don't move, don't talk, don't . . ." Miss Akana looked at Rosie and then at Apikalia, "don't do anything."

Rosie felt the teacher's disappointment. She stared at her hands, then pleated her skirt between her fingers, let it pop loose and pleated it again.

"Ah, Rosie Schatzer," said Mrs. Smith.

Looking up, Rosie saw Aunt Yvonne's friend standing in front of her, her arms folded across her chest. "Miss Akana tells me she is surprised at your behavior, but I am not." She turned to Apikalia, looked her up and down and simply motioned for her to follow. Rosie stood, but Mrs. Smith turned sharply. "Not you," she said. "I will deal with you once I find out what happened."

Why had she let herself lose control like that? Rosie had never physically fought with anyone in her life. She'd always depended on her words, but this time it was words that had driven her to act—Nazi, kraut, hun, enemy. None of those words were her.

It seemed like forever before Mrs. Smith and Apikalia came out of the principal's office. One thought that plagued Rosie as she waited was how ashamed her parents would be if they knew what she had done. For that she was sorry. The other was that this would not look good on her Punahou application.

Mrs. Smith patted Apikalia on the shoulder as she left. The girl did not even glance toward Rosie. Mrs. Smith motioned for Rosie to come into the office and she slowly obeyed.

Rosie had tried to come up with an explanation for her behavior as she'd waited for her turn to see Mrs. Smith. "Apikalia and her friends were very disrespectful toward me," she began.

Mrs. Smith held up her hand. "I don't want to hear one of your made-up stories. I know what you are capable of, how you behaved toward the kind woman who took you in when you needed a home."

Rosie had no idea what Mrs. Smith meant. She'd always respected Aunt Etta. Then she remembered. Aunt Yvonne had introduced her and Freddie as refugees when they had met Mrs. Smith the first time.

"You mean my Aunt Yvonne?"

"She even let you call her aunt!" Mrs. Smith said.

"Because she *is* my aunt. Yes, Yvonne Bell is my German aunt, my mother's sister. Her maiden name is Rauschling. And I'm not making up that story."

Mrs. Smith cleared her throat and glared at Rosie.

Uh-oh. She hadn't improved her situation with the principal. But Rosie took a small satisfaction at finally standing up against Aunt Yvonne's prejudice against her own family.

"Physically attacking another student is clearly a serious offense at this school."

"I was provoked!" Rosie said, always glad to be able to use a word she mostly only read in books. P-R-O-V-O-K-E-D.

"They were teasing you," Mrs. Smith said, dismissing Apikalia's and her friend's actions.

"*Teasing?*" Rosie couldn't believe her ears.

"You completely overreacted."

"Overreacted?"

"Am I not making myself clear?" Mrs. Smith asked. "Perhaps you will understand this. I have called your aunt, since your parents are clearly unavailable."

Rosie felt like she'd been struck again and this time by someone who should have known better.

"And she will arrive any minute to take you home for the next three school days."

"I'm suspended?" For three days? But the spelling bee was scheduled for Monday! And she wouldn't be allowed back in school until Wednesday.

"Fighting is an automatic suspension."

"Is Apikalia suspended?"

"Of course not! You attacked her. You may wait for your aunt out there. I will want to speak with her before she takes you home. You are dismissed."

Rosie couldn't believe what she was hearing. She had never been in trouble before and Apikalia had been the one to egg her into the fight. Aunt Etta was going to be so mad. She'd have to leave work and lose wages. And, she'd be very disappointed in how Rosie had handled the situation.

At the door, with her back turned to Mrs. Smith, Rosie gathered the courage to ask, "What about the spelling bee?"

"That," said the principal, "is a privilege and one you will be denied."

The words felt like a knife cutting through Rosie.

It seemed like Aunt Etta entered the waiting area of the office at the same moment Rosie did. Aunt Etta said nothing to her but walked to Mrs. Smith's door and rapped softly, then disappeared behind that door.

Rosie waited, still not sorry for what she did to Apikalia but very sorry that she'd caused Aunt Etta more trouble.

Aunt Etta still said nothing when she left Mrs. Smith's office. She walked by Rosie, who stood up as soon as the office door opened and fell into line behind her. They walked silently to the house.

Rosie sat on the sagging couch and waited as Aunt Etta paced back and forth across the small living room.

"If I drank, I think I would pour myself a healthy dose of something right now," were her aunt's first words. "And to think I've even given up cigarettes. I could use one of those right now also."

"I'm really sorry," Rosie said.

"It's embarrassing, what you did, and exactly the way people believe Germans are apt to behave—with violence and force. You've seen the propaganda posters, the big boots stomping down on Europe, and all the others."

Rosie hadn't even considered that she was acting the way Apikalia hoped or expected her to act.

"But I'm not German," Rosie said for the millionth time. "I have a German name. At some time in the past people from my family lived in Germany. I have never even been there. I am 100 percent American." Why, why, why couldn't people accept that?

"I know, but right now, oh my dear one, you have to act nobly, act better than others no matter what. I've heard it all, even from those I thought were my friends, the suspicion, the thoughtless comments, the hate, and the fear. Fear is driving so much of what people feel. Did you know that Apikalia's brother is in Europe fighting against the Nazis? He faces the worst of what Germany has to offer every single day."

"I didn't know that." Rosie felt a little seed of sorry for what she'd done to Apikalia.

Aunt Etta sat in the chair across from Rosie.

"I didn't think anyone knew about Mama and Papa and, you know, the internment. I was trying to defend our family honor."

Aunt Etta slowly nodded.

"You know and I know they didn't do anything wrong, but people who don't know them assume that because they were arrested and interned they did do something. It's not fair." Rosie shook her head until her hair covered her face and she had to push it out of the way.

"I think I know that even better than you do."

Of course she did.

"I know that being suspended is punishment," Aunt Etta began.

Not really, Rosie thought. *I don't care if I never go back to that school.* Missing the spelling bee was the real punishment.

"But, I have to follow that up with punishment here at home. I promised Mrs. Smith I would. So, you can't go to the beach or to town or anyplace out of the yard—"

"What if Iolana needs me to babysit?"

"Or Iolana's yard for the next three days."

Rosie watched her aunt pick at the strings on the frayed edges of the chair. Aunt Etta understood why she'd done what she'd done, she was sure of it.

"But, we're supposed to visit Mama at Sand Island on Sunday," Rosie said. Today was Friday and she couldn't go back to school until Wednesday. "Do Saturday and Sunday count?"

Aunt Etta swallowed hard. She nodded. "You won't be allowed to go with us this time."

Rosie gasped. "But . . ."

"No. And I don't relish telling her why you aren't along." Aunt Etta crossed her arms and looked down. Her lips quivered.

"Please," Rosie said quietly.

Aunt Etta stood and turned her back. "I am going back to work. I can still put in a few hours before the end of the day." And she was gone.

Chapter 35

Rosie stabbed her needle into her quilt square, thinking of Aunt Etta as she did so. Her aunt and Freddie were on their way to Sand Island to visit Mama.

One more row of quilting and the square would be finished, or almost finished. The edges needed to be finished, but Rosie wasn't sure how to do that. She'd planned to ask Mama to help her during this visit.

The rain pounded the roof of their house, sounding like it might break through it at any moment. And Rosie felt the thunder. It reminded her of bombs dropping on December 7, a date which will live in infamy. She tied off the last stitch.

Usually Rosie liked to be alone, but knowing where Aunt Etta and Freddie had gone and who they were seeing, she felt lonely and sad—and mad. At herself and at her aunt. She couldn't even write in her journal because George had taken it to review what she'd found out about Mr. Smith.

And next week, Rosie had to return to school—the school where Mrs. Smith and Apikalia were. Rosie felt like she could expect nothing from the principal in the way of protection from Apikalia's mean spirit. And the spelling bee would be over. She'd never be champion anything.

Rosie covered her face with the quilt square. She'd had too many bad thoughts as she was finishing it and had probably destroyed its aloha spirit, if it had ever had any. She threw the square to the floor. Kealani had said by the time she finished the quilting, Mama and Papa would return, and there was no sign of either. Was there any aloha spirit left on the islands or had it all blown up and away with the bombs?

Rosie stood in front of the screen door and let the wind and stray raindrops pound around her. She opened the door and stepped onto the front stoop. The rain quickly soaked through her dress, cooling her. Rosie ran to the tall pine tree in Iolana's yard and shimmied up the trunk until she reached a perch near the very top.

She imagined she could see across the water to the tents of Sand Island, where Mama, Aunt Etta, and Freddie would be wading through the rain from the dinner hall to the dock. Rosie shivered more with loneliness than with cold. She wanted her mama and her papa. And she sobbed. For the first time since Aunt Etta had been taken away, Rosie cried and cried and cried.

"Rosie! Are you out here?" Aunt Etta called.

Rosie stayed where she was, not ready to face anyone. Perhaps she'd stay in the tree all night and even tomorrow and the day after and the day after. That way she wouldn't have to go to school.

"Rosie! *Liebchen!*"

Rosie wondered if she was finally losing her mind. It sounded like her mother's voice.

"Roselie!"

That voice sounded like her father's. She couldn't hear her papa all the way from the mainland and as far as she knew, that was where he was.

Rosie climbed down carefully, looking over her shoulder every few feet to see if it was Mama and Papa or her mind playing tricks.

But, standing there, drenched in rain, were her parents. They looked as wet as she felt, and their clothes, the ones they'd been wearing way back in early December, hung on them. Papa's hair was shorter than she remembered and Mama's was tied back with a scarf. Papa looked like the handsomest man she'd ever seen, and her mama the most beautiful woman. Freddie roosted in Papa's arms as Mama paced from one side of the muddy yard to the other.

"Mama? Papa?" Rosie stood under the pine branches, still not sure if she was awake or dreaming. "Papa, when did you return?"

Mama ran to her and held her tightly. "What are you doing out here in the pouring rain?"

"What are *you* doing out here?" Rosie asked. "I was watching for you to come home. If I look very, very hard, I can see Sand Island and your tent."

"Is it empty?"

Rosie nodded.

"That's because we're home!" Mama said. "Me *and* your papa."

Chapter 36

Mama and Papa still had no explanation for why they had been interned, and no explanation for why they had been released, no matter how many questions Rosie asked. Papa had returned from Wisconsin on the mainland and joined Mama at Sand Island. They had been called to the superintendent's office and told that like Aunt Etta, they were "paroled." She finally gave up and decided she'd have to be content with her own explanations.

Mama did not make Freddie go to school the next day. Rosie was still suspended.

"You'll have to stay here while we take care of some business," Papa said after they had eaten a coconut breakfast.

Rosie didn't want to let her parents out of her sight so soon. "Why can't we go with you?"

"I want to come, too!" Freddie whined.

Mama and Papa exchanged looks. "It will be very boring for you," Papa said.

"You will have to be very patient while you wait for us, so perhaps you should take a book," said Mama, giving in easily. Rosie figured Mama didn't want to be separated from them any more than she and Freddie did.

Rosie grabbed a book and Freddie shoved several plastic planes and army men into his pockets.

"So where are we going?" Rosie held on to Papa's hand and Freddie held tightly to Mama's as they made their way toward town.

"To see a Mr. Weinstein, a friend of Aunt Etta's George," Papa said. "We are going to have to find another place to live."

Papa bringing up Mr. Weinstein's name made Rosie wonder what had happened to her journal. She'd returned to writing notes on any paper she could find as she had done at Aunt Yvonne's. She hoped George hadn't lost her real journal.

"Our properties have not been managed the way we expected," Papa continued. "In fact, we've lost our house in the valley."

"I know," Rosie paused, trying to decide how much to tell her parents of what she knew. "Malia bought the house and is running a nursery there."

Mama and Papa exchanged looks.

"She was probably the one who made a report about you to the FBI to make sure you were interned," Rosie continued, "then she could have the house."

"We don't know that, *liebchen*," Papa said.

"But I think it," said Rosie. She had failed to truly be like Nancy Drew—she hadn't solved the mystery of the cause of her parents' internment. She only had theories. But it was impossible, with all the secrecy, to know anything for sure! The FBI might not even know who made the report on Mama and Papa if it was anonymous.

"You are free to think what you like. But you may not go around accusing people when you don't *know*."

Rosie opened her mouth to speak but Papa shushed her. "We are better than that," he said. "We must go now and find a place to live. A place fit for a princess!"

"Please, Papa, no more princess. I think I have outgrown that title."

Papa looked at her, tears in his eyes. "I am sorry for that." He put his arm around Rosie and they walked on together.

"We are hopeful to recover our remaining properties including the Diamond Head house and move there," Papa said. "It is small but it belongs to us. And it is not as small as this house."

Rosie checked on Mama and Freddie who followed more slowly. Freddie was pointing at things and talking nonstop as Mama nodded and smiled.

"Mr. Smith said he'd rented it to the government when we told him we wanted to live there," Rosie told Papa.

"As I said, Mr. Smith hasn't been quite the manager we had in mind for our properties."

"He took things from our house and he's been selling them," Rosie said.

"Again, we cannot accuse people of theft when we don't know—"

Rosie interrupted him. "I saw him take quilts, one Auntie Palu gave us, to a store and sell them. And Kam, he's one of our new friends, he said Mr. Smith was there when the government men took all the radios from your store."

"*Liebchen*, I will not be selling radios again. At least not while this war carries on." Papa shook his head and his shoulders slumped.

"But you're the radio king . . ."

"No longer. They do not trust me with radios." He placed a finger over his lips and Rosie quieted.

They walked along, dodging soldiers and sandbags, Papa looking this way and that. "Changes, so many," he mumbled.

Papa stopped suddenly and Rosie stumbled. "Ah! This is the office we seek." He pushed open the door and held it while Rosie, then Mama and Freddie entered.

A thin man with dark hair and round rimmed glasses stood at the desk staring at stacks of papers. He looked up as they came inside.

"Mr. Weinstein?" Papa said.

"You must be Mr. and Mrs. Schatzer!" Weinstein stepped from behind the desk and shook first Papa's then Mama's hand.

"Are you Rosie?" he asked.

Rosie couldn't imagine how he knew her name.

"I'm George's friend and he talks about you and your brother often," Weinstein explained.

Rosie hoped it was good talk. She hoped George hadn't mentioned her fight at school.

"In fact, I've used your diary to track some of the actions of your property manager."

Mama and Papa both turned to look at Rosie.

Rosie didn't know what to say.

"And I was able to make a strong enough case that Mr. Smith has been removed and I have been appointed in his place."

"That is wonderful news." Papa shook Mr. Weinstein's hand vigorously. "Wonderful."

"Thank you so much! That does mean that the remainder of our properties will not be sold, correct?" Mama asked, wringing her hands.

"I could not save the valley home, but I have managed to stop any further action on the Diamond Head house, the storefront off King Street, and the other pieces of land you own in the hills. And, I fear, I cannot recover any personal property that seems to be missing."

"We must be content with what we still have," Mama said.

Mr. Weinstein turned to Mama and Papa. "I have heard reports of some of the managers profiting from their not-so-honest activities, but they do have signed authority from you to manage the property. There isn't much we can do."

Rosie knew he was right, no matter how much she wanted

to make sure Mr. Smith never took advantage of another family.

"We don't want to make any trouble or bring any attention to ourselves," Papa said in a low voice as he stood between Rosie and Mr. Weinstein. "We must keep our heads down and make it through these different days."

Being with her parents again, Rosie realized having her family together was more important to her than bringing Mr. Smith to the justice he deserved.

"There were others we talked to when we were . . ." Mama paused, "interned." She swallowed hard. "They, too, had no chance to pack or store personal belongings and now," she snapped her fingers, "their things have disappeared."

"I do have some understanding of what you've been through. I, like George, am Jewish. If we were in Germany, we would be the ones picked up for no reason except our heritage and placed in camps. Although, from what I have heard, the camps there are far worse and fewer people find their way out alive than the people interned here." Mr. Weinstein picked up papers and shuffled through them, not looking at the Schatzers.

"It is a shame and a stain on Germany," Papa finally said.

Weinstein dropped the papers on the desk and gave the family a wan smile. "No one seems to want to help the Jews in Europe either."

"When do you think we will be able to take back our house near Diamond Head?" Mama asked.

"Soon. I have already notified the renters they will have to move."

"But doesn't the government have the lease on the house?" Rosie asked, sure that's what Mr. Smith had said.

"Mr. Smith's cousin is living there presently." Mr. Weinstein pressed his lips together.

"We are very grateful for all your help," said Papa.

"It is my job. I spend my days trying to help internees and I'm glad I could help you." He pulled out a brown envelope from under the many papers stacked on his desk. "Rosie, this is yours. And this as well."

Rosie opened the envelope—her Christmas journal! And Mr. Weinstein also handed her a brand new journal with a red, white, and blue cover. "Thank you," she whispered, stroking the cover.

"You deserve it," he said. "As I said, your notes were most helpful in tracking Mr. Smith's movements and his selling off of personal property belonging to internees."

"We will hear from you when the house is available?" Papa asked.

"Soon," replied Mr. Weinstein. "And I will also give you an accounting of funds due you and an inventory of any personal property and real estate I can locate."

After another round of thank-yous, Rosie and her parents left the office.

"I feel much better," said Papa, stretching his arms to the sky.

"And I will feel better when we find work," said Mama.

"The shop is still there. I went to see it . . ."

"Rosie, the government will not let me work with radios just as they will not let Etta have her cameras again," said Papa. "There is fear we will give secrets to the Germans. They do not believe with our German blood and German name we can be loyal Americans."

"But now, we shall eat ice cream and celebrate being with our *kinder* once again," Mama said, putting an arm around Rosie and the other around Freddie. "That is what matters."

Rosie hadn't had ice cream since the war began and she could already taste it as they headed toward the nearest restaurant.

Once the family had their ice cream, Papa led them to a nearby park where they sat near a Banyan tree so broad and twisted, Rosie thought an entire family could move in and make their home. She relaxed and soaked in the sunlight and warmth of being with her family.

"There is one other thing Papa and I want to discuss with you," Mama said, licking her ice cream cone and looking at Papa, not Rosie or Freddie.

Rosie tensed.

"Mama and I would like to ask you, both of you but especially you, Rosie, to not bring up the subject of our internment again. No questions, no discussion, no more talk about it . . ."

"But Papa, don't you want to know why?" Rosie asked, not able to understand how he could push the worst thing that had ever happened to them into the background and act like it had never happened.

"We accept that it did happen. We believe it happened because we were German and because people grow afraid in times of war. And we, your mama and I, choose to let it go. We must pick up our bootstraps, go forward, and achieve."

"There must be a reason . . ."

"Rosie, for your papa and I, please, we want no more said. Lock it away. Forget about it. It is over and done."

For Mama and Papa, Rosie would try, but there would always be a part of her seeking an explanation, a part of her that wanted to know.

Chapter 37

Rosie's schoolbag was heavy with books. Her new teacher was big on homework. It had been hard to leave her new friends behind and change to yet a third school when the family moved to the house near Diamond Head. The move did mean she didn't have to see either Apikalia or Mrs. Smith every day.

Even before she opened the door to the house, Rosie heard laughter coming from inside. Auntie Palu had come to visit!

Before Rosie could drop her schoolbag, Auntie Palu had her wrapped in a warm hug. "Auntie! Leilani! I am so glad to see you! How are the boys?"

"Oh, they worry me! Both my boys are on a ship in the ocean, fighting the Japs. They thought to join the Army but decided it would be impossible to live away from the water and enlisted in the Navy instead. They are very brave."

"I told Auntie to leave their addresses with us and we would write them letters," Mama said.

"They would love to hear from you! And little Freddie, they asked me if he had learned to surf yet."

"He has! Our friend, Kam, taught him. Freddie is so good! Me, not so good." Rosie laughed. It felt so familiar to be chatting with Auntie.

"Your friend Kam, eh?" Leilani teased. "Is he also helping you study for the big spelling championship coming up?"

"I was hoping we could do that together," Rosie said. She'd easily won the spelling bee at her newest school and would be competing against her friend at the championship. But they'd agreed they'd be happy if either of them won, so long as the winner was one of them.

"I brought you haupia and poi and pork from our luau. You must miss our Hawaiian foods!"

"Not the poi," Rosie said honestly and Auntie laughed.

"You said when you no longer were needed to watch Freddie, you would come with us to the Army base to serve food and aloha spirit to the boys there," Auntie Palu reminded her. "I am holding you to that."

"It's fun," said Leilani. "They all want to dance!"

"I'm a terrible dancer," said Rosie.

"So are most of them!"

"I'll try," said Rosie.

"We will pick you up on Saturday," said Auntie Palu. "Wear your dancing shoes!"

"Auntie brought some other things you might be interested in as well," Mama said. "I will let her show you while I go check on the *kinder*." She rolled her eyes. Rosie knew Mama had her hands full with the little ones she cared for every day in the new kindergarten she'd opened.

"Your mama showed me your quilting. You are doing beautiful work," said Auntie Palu. "I am very proud of you."

"I like doing it. And we have to replace the quilts we lost when . . ." Rosie made herself say nothing else.

Auntie nodded as she picked up a large basket and pulled out a piece of paper. "Fill this out," she said.

Rosie read the paper. "Auntie Palu, I'm not good enough to enter a quilting contest!"

"You are. I have an application for your mama, too. And I will also enter. But in an advanced category."

"I'll think about it," Rosie promised. If she did win, it was something to add to her Punahou application, a champion of something not many other students could claim.

"And what about this," said Auntie Palu. She pulled a quilt out of the basket. The colors and the fabric reminded Rosie of the Queen's quilt, but it couldn't be.

"I visited my friend at the Royal Hawaiian Quilt Shop in downtown Honolulu to buy supplies. And what do I see hanging on the wall? Your mama's Queen's quilt! I know it is," Auntie said excitedly, "because who helped your mama sew that crazy quilt? Auntie Palu did.

"I say to my friend, that is not your quilt! She tell me she buy it fair and square and I argue that it was taken from my beloved neighbor, my favorite mama of Rosie and Freddie, and I know because my aloha spirit is in that quilt!"

Rosie could hear and see Auntie in her mind scolding the woman in the quilt shop. She *had* seen Auntie do the same thing in fact when she saved their Hawaiian quilt.

"And I reach up and unpin that quilt and fold it up. I throw some money on the counter and bring it home with me. I am happy to return it to you." Auntie sat back and wiped a line of sweat off her forehead.

Rosie spread the quilt on the floor and examined it carefully. It had a few splotches of dirt and was missing some key new experiences the family had undergone, but she was thrilled to have it back where it belonged.

Rosie heard another sound, a faint mew and looked at Auntie's basket. "Is that . . . did you find . . ." She crawled over to the basket and peered inside. There was a tiny orange ball of fluff trying to climb out.

"I wish I could bring you Kitty but she has never come back," Auntie said, placing a hand on Rosie's shoulder. "But another young cat showed up under our porch and gave birth to seven babies. Can you imagine? Seven babies at one time! And this one, this littlest one," Auntie pulled the kitten out and rubbed it against her cheek, "told me she wanted to live with Rosie."

Rosie swallowed hard. It wasn't Kitty but the little orange fluffball was so adorable. It mewed and seemed to scrabble toward Rosie.

"See," said Auntie, "she knows she belongs with you."

"I can't call her Kitty," Rosie said. "Maybe Coconut?" She cuddled the kitten and her heart melted as its rough tongue licked her hand. Auntie was right, Coconut belonged to her.

"Thank you, Auntie, for everything," said Rosie.

"I feel bad," she said, "for not helping more when your mama and papa were taken. I come over to your house and you were gone. I didn't know where until you came to visit that day. I wish you had come to us."

"You have so many people at your house . . ."

"There will always be room for you," Auntie said. "I hope you do not need me again like that, but if you do, I will be very angry if you do not come to me."

"Thank you, Auntie." Rosie continued to cuddle the kitten.

A loud knock sounded on the door. Rosie and Coconut jumped up to answer it. Every time she heard someone at the door, it brought back a tinge of fear that the government men had returned. The fear grew less and less but it hadn't gone away yet. She was relieved to see Kam's face pressed against the screen.

"Thought I'd come by and say hi. Hey, is that your cat?" he greeted her.

"This is Coconut, not Kitty, but she's pretty cute, isn't she? And so cuddly!" Rosie let Kam inside and handed him the kitten.

Kam held it away from him as if he didn't know what to do with a cat.

"Pet her!" Rosie said, laughing as Kam patted Coconut's head with two fingers. She took the cat back.

"I can't believe a big, strong guy like you is afraid of a little kitten!" Leilani joined them, flipping her hair and smiling at Kam.

"Allergies," Kam said, "not afraid."

Hmm, Rosie thought. Looked like her old friend and her new friend might hit it off.

"I hear you're a surfer," Leilani said. "Bet I'm better."

"We'll have to see about that," Kam said. "Anytime."

A car pulled up and Rosie saw through the door Aunt Etta and George walking toward the house. It was turning into a party. Aunt Etta waved and pulled George up the sidewalk. "Where's your mother?" she called.

"Right here!" Mama entered, carrying Enya, the youngest of her charges.

"Is Henry around?"

Mama looked over Aunt Etta's shoulder, "Coming up the walk right now. Freddie, too."

The living room felt crowded once everyone was inside, all talking at once, trying to pet the kitten, and see the quilt. Auntie Palu hugged and kissed everyone as she greeted them and Freddie kept asking for some of the haupia she had brought.

Aunt Etta clapped her hands. "We have an announcement." She held up her left hand.

Rosie saw a small diamond ring sparkling on her ring finger.

"We're getting married!" Aunt Etta said proudly. She leaned against George.

"Congratulations!"

"You must have the wedding at our house. And a luau!" Auntie said.

"We can't impose like that," Aunt Etta said. "We'll go to city hall."

"You must!" Auntie insisted.

Rosie looked at the faces surrounding her, each one familiar and loving, not different at all. The war was there and looked like it would be looming for some time, but she had so much else to look forward to. Perhaps she would learn to dance. Perhaps Aunt Etta would ask her to be a bridesmaid when she married George. Perhaps she would become a champion at something! It was time to turn her different days into good days.

Historical Note

Different Days is inspired by a true story and real events, specifically the story of a girl named Doris Berg.

Doris Berg (right) and her sister Anita in 1940.

On December 7, 1941, eleven-year-old Doris Berg watched Japanese planes rain bombs on Pearl Harbor from her home in the Nuuanu Valley, Honolulu, Oahu, Territory of Hawaii.

Even through the smoke, noise, and uproar of the attack, Doris felt safe because her family was there to care for her.

The next day, everything changed. Doris's father, Fred Berg, went to his job at Sears while her mother, Bertha Berg, stayed home to take care of patients still in residence at the nursing home they ran. The nursing home comprised the first two stories of the home where they lived on the third floor. Late in the morning of December 8, Federal Bureau of Investigation (FBI) agents arrived at the home/business and took Mrs. Berg away to "ask her some questions," leaving Doris in charge of her younger sister and the few remaining patients. Most patients had been removed by family because of the bombing. Neither Mr. nor Mrs. Berg returned that evening. Doris had no idea where they were, why they had been taken, or what was happening to them. She thought the worst.

The islands of Hawaii had been placed under martial law as a result of the bombing. Schools were closed and blackouts imposed. Grocery stores were ordered to close for inventory and subsequent rationing because shipments of food from the mainland were interrupted. News was censored and citizens had to abide by a curfew. The military was in charge.

During the first week at the nursing home without her parents, Doris, still in charge, struggled mightily with what was happening. Strangers walked in and out of her house. Some were FBI agents searching for and seizing contraband (cameras, binoculars, radios, flashlights, anything that could be used to signal or communicate with the enemy). Others she believed to be relatives of patients taking them out of the home and others simply helped themselves to whatever they desired from the cabinets and furnishings of the Berg home.

After a week on their own, Doris's and Anita's older sister, Eleanor, arrived and took some of the pressure off Doris—temporarily. The FBI showed up yet again and took Eleanor to ask her questions, leaving the young sisters abandoned again. Eleanor was allowed to call the day she was taken to assure Doris and Anita that she was all right but she was unable to offer any additional information in the short phone conversation.

Doris's aunt, her mother's older sister, first hired a nurse to care for the girls. But by late December, with still no word from their parents, they had moved to their aunt's home. They were cautioned to not mention the whereabouts of their parents (which they didn't know anyway) and their aunt introduced them as refugees.

At her aunt's, Doris also met Mr. Reed, a local realtor appointed to manage her parents' properties, for the first time in late December. He brought several gifts for the girls that he had recovered from their home at the request of their parents. He drove Doris and Anita to the house to pack clothes and other belongings but the house had been stripped bare. Doris's cat, Kitty Poo, met her at the door, but her aunt refused to allow her to bring the cat with her. That was the last time she saw Kitty Poo, another loss.

On Christmas Day, the celebration was low key—a makeshift tree, no carols, none of the German traditions the girls loved. Every trace of German heritage had to be erased and ignored so long as their aunt felt the family was under surveillance for possible anti-American activities. Their aunt let them have the gifts of clothing their parents had sent, but insisted the remaining gifts be donated to the Salvation Army.

In January 1942, Doris and Anita finally received a letter—snuck out by a released prisoner—from their mother telling them that she was well and being held at Fort Armstrong, interned as an enemy alien.

Doris couldn't understand. Her parents and her sister were neither enemies nor aliens (noncitizens living in the United States). Her mother and Eleanor had been born in Hawaii, making them lifelong American citizens. Her father had proudly become a naturalized citizen in 1940. It had to be a mistake! Once the officials realized her parents and Eleanor were American citizens, they would surely be released.

Unknown to Doris, her family members had already been given hearings in front of a three-man board but were not informed of the charges made against them or who had made those charges. This made it impossible for them to respond. This was the accepted practice for dealing with internees. The hearing was a courtesy only. The Bergs had also been coerced into signing statements they did not agree with. The fact of their citizenship was ignored.

In February 1942, Mrs. Berg and Eleanor were transferred to what the Bergs referred to as a concentration camp on Sand Island in Honolulu Harbor. Mr. Berg was shipped with other male internees to Fort McCoy, Wisconsin.

In April, Eleanor was paroled and took over care of Doris and Anita after their aunt suffered a heart attack, saving them from having to go into an orphanage. Their father returned from the mainland and was reunited with their mother. The girls were finally allowed to visit them at Sand Island.

Living with Eleanor was a release from life with their prim and proper aunt, but conditions were tough. Mr. Reed claimed there was no money available for the girls' support and by caring for her sisters, Eleanor was violating her parole. The girls learned to lie because it was the most important thing in the world to stay together.

Eventually, Mr. and Mrs. Berg were sent to Camp Honouliuli in the Waianae Mountains. The camp was located in a gulch with little relief from the heat. The girls were, however, now permitted to visit for the weekend twice a month until their mother's parole in June 1943 and their father's in August 1943.

Fred, Bertha, and Eleanor were three of the 10,905 Germans interned at various locations throughout the United States during World War II.

The genesis of the internment process began in the late 1930s when President Franklin Roosevelt and FBI director J. Edgar Hoover created a secret intelligence network to identify people in the United States who might be a threat in the war they knew was on the horizon. This stemmed in part from lingering fear of the German community in World War I.

In response to this, a Custodial Detention Index was created, rating a person's degree of threat to safety from A (most dangerous) to C (least dangerous). Aliens were required to register, starting in 1940, and answer a series of questions that were kept on file.

Citizens were encouraged to report any suspicions of spying, sabotage, or unusual enemy-related activities to the FBI. These reports were often based on innuendo, hearsay, and gossip. The reports were confidential, often anonymous, and the evidence was seldom corroborated or investigated beyond the word of the informant.

Some of the people interned indeed were leaders in the Nazi party in the US (the Bund) and harbored strong patriotic ties to Germany, but others were interned solely because of perceived German sympathies. These might include things like membership in German organizations, listening to German music, subscribing to a German newspaper, or receiving mail from Germany. Gatherings, even social gatherings of ethnic Germans, and speaking German were also considered evidence of loyalty to Germany.

Little attention has been paid to the fact that thousands of Germans (and a smaller number of Italians) were interned in the US during World War II. Japanese internment and relocation is much more widely known and studied. Because of the relocation from the West Coast, many more Japanese spent the war in internment camps. Those Japanese who were interned also received an apology and compensation from the government. The German and other European internees have received neither.

Upon release, internees signed a form agreeing to not speak of their internment and many feared violating that agreement would lead to being incarcerated again. Others felt internment left a stain on their reputations whether they'd done anything wrong or not. These factors contributed to people not knowing what had happened.

No matter ethnicity, internment tore families apart, left children without parents to be cared for by relatives or orphanages, left wives and mothers without financial support, and left a lasting legacy of pain for families and internees to deal with.

For many years the Berg family did not speak of the internment years. And they did not know who had reported them or what had been reported. The informants were later found to be two patients from the nursing home who suffered from alcoholism and mental issues, a former disgruntled employee of the nursing home, and a coworker of Mr. Berg's. The family lost personal and real property, their business, and time as a family. Upon release, they had to start from scratch. Mr. Berg left his daughters with this lesson: "Only cowards give up, so pick up your bootstraps, move forward, and achieve."

Doris Berg did just that. She graduated from the prestigious Punahou School on Oahu, attended the University of Hawaii and UCLA, and became a teacher and counselor as well as a wife and mother. Doris has also worked tirelessly to spread information about the injustices of internment, specifically the little-known German internment, in hopes that knowledge will keep history from repeating.

For further information:

Estlack, Russell. *Shattered Lives, Shattered Dreams: The Untold Story of America's Enemy Aliens in World War II.* Salt Lake: Cedar Fort, 2011

Russell, Jan Jarboe. *The Train to Crystal City: FDR's Secret Prisoner Exchange Program and America's Only Family Internment Camp During World War II.* New York: Scribner, 2015.

Websites:

www.gaic.info. German American Internee Coalition.

www.foitimes.com. Freedom of Information Times.

Acknowledgments

This story, although fictionalized, was inspired by that of Doris Berg Nye, and I am extremely grateful to her for sharing her life as the daughter of interned German Americans in World War II Hawaii, as well as answering my many questions. It has been a blessing and a pleasure to become acquainted with her. Doris, you are one of my heroes! Thank you. And I hope, as you do, that knowledge of history will keep that history from repeating.

Thanks to Bethany Buck for recognizing *Different Days* as a story that needed to be told and helping me shape it. Thanks also to Alison Weiss, Sky Pony editorial director, for making me feel a part of the family, and thanks especially to Becky Herrick, Sky Pony editor, for her help and support to see the book through to completion.

The members of my Thursday writing group, Stephanie, Jeanie, Kristen, Valerie, Yvonne, Cindy and Peggy, have been invaluable in the feedback and suggestions they offered. Thank you ladies for always being there! And I'd like to mention and thank Norma Bentzinger for sharing her stories of her German family's experiences with prejudice during both wars.

And finally, to my family—the Lauzes, the young Erwins, and especially my husband, Jim—thanks for sharing the journey. I couldn't do it without you.